Long Time to Sunset

Don felt alone and troubled. His fear was tight with a call to action. He'd known this feeling the morning of Howard Taylor's funeral. The gray clouds seemed to signal his sense of concern as they streamed ever so slowly across the sky, towards him. There could not have been a better description for what they had done, or why. Don knew he would have to deal with it one day, and that time had come, as the moon was turning full, and a letter he would need to read was in a P.O. Box he no longer used.

After breakfast with Arleen, he walked over to Charlie's diner on 8th, just off to the side of the main road in an alleyway that people used as such. It was partly how Charles Riley got the license to open the restaurant, he had to allow tourist to eat at his place yet not require passersby to patronize it. Charlie had thought to wall off the patio, but customers preferred the openness while they ate to people watch and enjoy the island breezes.

Charlie and Don went back to the drug days, shooting those narcotics, and running the streets hustling every way they could. Both did some time but cleaned up in their early thirties. They went separate ways, established good lives, Charles as a small business procurement employee, and Don as a small business owner, courier services. Now, almost forty years later, an event that should have stayed buried, was about to be uncovered. He wasn't sure how Charlie was involved or would remember what happened. It was where he had to start to get some relief from the panic he felt.

Don turned seventy-two on Mother's Day. He felt good, Arleen was healthy again and they were planning a trip to New Mexico. Last year's trip had been postponed due to a recurrence of her illness that required a ten-day stay in the hospital. The treatment took and she was declared cured, and she looked it. She was able to return to work for six months before retiring and Don had thrown a big party at their house for friends and co-workers to embrace her transition and restoration of health. She sold the Art Supply company she had run for twenty-five

1

years, and the new owners kept the seven employees who had worked for her. It was a good deal and a good time. She knew about his past relationship with Charlie and what he felt he needed to do. She was not supportive but accepted his reasoning. She just hoped it wouldn't interfere with their beach trip before going out west.

*

Howard Taylor no longer lived on Oliver Street, he had moved into a retirement village eighty miles east of Atlanta and was using the name Tyler Johnson, a counselor he had known years ago. He was glad time was moving on so nicely and the regrets were not as strong these days. He missed the old days and the freedoms he had earned, but anonymity had its place. The events that caused the deception were far removed and retirement was feeling good. The only problem was that Don Maynard had tried to contact him by way of social media using Tyler's real name. He did not respond and hoped Don would give up the hunt. Don could be trouble if he were trying to excavate things that needed to remain buried. Those things happened a long time ago.

*

Charlotte Rainey was in hospice and had been given her final prayers. She was day to day and had not spoken to anyone since Tuesday. It was Friday and she was alone. Staff had been wonderful the past two weeks, and she had expressed her gratitude for their care of her. She had maintained a pleasant smile though in pain from liver failure and seemed at peace with how it was ending. One of the nuns found the letter addressed to a Don Maynard in the bible that was on the nightstand next to her bed. She had passed sometime early Saturday morning.

*

"Charles Linwood Riley, good to see you," spoke Don as he entered the diner, looking around, nodding to guests as if he owned the place. "Wow, man you look good," he expressed to his old friend as they embraced and shook hands. "Man, the place looks great!"

"Don Maynard, my friend, how the hell are you?" Charlie shot back, maintaining the hug before pushing back giving Don a forceful slap of the palm of his left hand. "Man, oh man, oh man, sweet Jesus, you look good yourself. Man, we're still here!"

"Yeah," Don says, turning his head side to side, as if in disbelief himself. "Yeah man, we're still here, wow!"

"Come on, let's go sit down over here, away from the street," Charlie says, gesturing to his left.

The dining area was small, maybe four hundred square feet, but could hold twenty-two people comfortably when the two-seater tables were arranged properly. Of course, there would be times during each of the three daily meals when they would have to be adjusted to handle a group but that was generally not a problem with a beach crowd.

Charlie had been here about six years now and things were good. He had a good staff, and his wife Regina would come pitch in every once and again. They served the basic food groups and customers could come and go with ease. There was no pretense here, good food, good service, "Tell your friends; Come back when you're in town!"

Don continued to work the crowd with his eyes before sitting, taking note of one grandmother who winked at him. It calmed him down and he returned his attention to his old pal.

"Man, this is great," Don says, reaching out both hands to join them with Charlie's who mirrors the move. "Man, we are still here, we have been blessed!"

"So, what brings you here?" Charlie asks after motioning for the bar person to bring over some waters.

"Arleen just retired, and we're headed out to New Mexico. We wanted to get a few days of beach first and I found out about your place here. We usually go over to Hilton Head."

"Nice."

"Well, you know, got to do it, right?"

"True. So, what's been going on?" Charlie asks.

Don looks around to catch a moment of privacy and softly mentions, "Howard Taylor is still alive."

"You're kidding," Charlie almost shouts, causing a couple to look over at them. "Let's go back into the office area," Charlie says to Don and smiles at the couple.

*

Howard Taylor was still a sharp dresser, not fine, just nice, and neat, current, leather shoes, twill pants, starched shirts, and a good cap atop his head. Of course, he always took the hat off indoors. He had good facial features, still an athlete's body though slowed by age and stress. At seventy-four, still a gentleman's greeting to all with comfortable handshakes and a wink of the eye. He had settled nicely into Parson's Retirement Village and was popular but not too forth coming about his past life. He generally said "investor' when asked about his life's work. Finding out that he was single two ladies had already tried to claim him, but he remained cordial to all. He felt he had too much dark history for this crowd of good people and gentle spirits, though several residents could probably match him regarding secrecy of actions. A few agents of various persuasions were residents, and several retired military personnel. Tyler Johnson, as it were, fit right in as many were carrying secrets to the grave.

His unit was a fair size six-hundred square feet, the price was right, and he had a clear view of the courtyard and the path that led to the serenity garden. He had brought over furnishings from the last house he sold, and he was very comfortable. He had taken to writing stories again, jotting down impressions of his new life and the people and events that came his way. It was nice to chart the present, and not try and interpret the past. He thought of Charlotte though and the old gang on occasion, but those memories were becoming fewer and less pleasant as time went on. His new life was more rewarding and satisfying without the treachery of old. He felt blessed that he had no major illnesses nor too much trauma from the old days. That was a different life. Drug dealing and illegal hustling had made him wealthy, but that career still carried a burden that he would not be relieved of as long as certain folks were still alive. Necessary things had been done that were painful to recall and that could still land him in the penitentiary.

*

Charlie's office was just a walk-in closet basically, 5' x 6'. Records for supplies and such, journals and magazines were on a small desk, with a laptop and printer present. The two chairs were tidy, and Don felt cramped as he tried to relax just enough. Charlie's face showed concern and fear, and he nervously knocked a paper cup to the floor, fortunately it was empty. Don pulled the envelope from his back pocket and pulled the letter out.

"Should I read this, or do you want to just talk for a minute?" he asked Charlie.

"Let's just talk a bit first, this is not at all what I expected for today's events. What happened to Charlotte, and where is Howard?" Charlie spoke, almost as if he were talking to the walls.

"This is a strange letter, written in a strange way. Charlotte died in hospice six months ago and she had left it in a bible. The note from the nun said she had left instructions on the outside of the envelope with my name and the address of my old P.O. Box. It had been sitting in there because I don't use it anymore. I closed it two weeks ago. That's when I found it. Must have been cancer or something, I had not heard from her in years, right before she went back to prison, fifteen years or so. I don't know how she survived that long. She may have been sixty-eight. Howard kept her up all those years, but she was just wayward. She couldn't stay out of those streets. Howard just, you know, I guess they used each other. Anyway, I don't know."

"Didn't she work for you for a while as a driver?" Charlie asks him.

"I'd give her a few small deliveries, you know, but she couldn't be trusted," Don shared.

"She was hard, grew up hard," Charlie recalled. "So, Howard?"

"I don't know what to say. It's stuff out there that's been buried a long time. If he's still living, I don't know what to expect," Don presented. "Let me just read you the letter. The first part was crossed out, but this is what she wrote:"

GOOSE BUMPS ON THE WINDOW

Hey Don. Anyway, this is for you.

He did not call back and I was restless. I was on my own again. Chuck and Larry were dead, and Sonny was back in prison, this time for life. My secret was safe for now. I walked two miles to the train station and bought a ticket for Shady Dale. I had to get back home even though it had been thirty years since I left. The cold air had opened my sinuses, and my focus was restored. I had to get to a safe place before I had to answer any questions. I was trained to do certain things, and he had paid me well. It was probably good that he had not called back as promised. I needed to get away from him.

"Then she goes on."

The ride was smooth and easy, and I slept most of the three-hundred miles. The motions and train sounds were like a sedative to me whether the steel on steel or the people moving about; and the creaky squeaks and the circular rocking of the car helped me rest even though I was disturbed by what had happened. I just knew I felt okay if we were moving.

Shady Dale, unlike the name, was a bustling, bright small-town south of Savannah. I was raised in a good section, where our grandparents moved to in the early 1920's, bought homes, worked, and raised those large families. Coal was stored in the basement and the young men opened the traps early in the mornings and shoveled the day's supply for the fireplaces those few times in the winter. I suppose it was a tough, gritty existence, but what I heard them talk about mostly was the getting through it, the people and experiences that come to make a life worthwhile.

Leaving the station, and not knowing where to begin, I hailed a cab to get a tour of the area. I did not know what it would look like, nor did I have a clue as to who was still around. Too many of my friends were dead long ago, and the ones who had survived had moved on to other parts of the city. Usually by forty-five most folks were settled into the life they had chosen, and circumstances were less important.

I asked the cab driver to go over near the graveyard where my formative years were spent. I thought that a good place to start as I could replay events and experiences that became crucial to my 'career path.' The closer we got the more the area was like a war zone, roofs and parts of walls were missing from apartment buildings, debris and stale human smells filled the air, memories of acts best left hidden flooded my consciousness, and I was somewhere I could not imagine.

"I think I know you," the driver spoke when he sensed I had come to a wrong place.

"You're Howard's sister aren't you, the one who served it up all that time?"

I looked around and almost asked him to stop and let me out of the cab, but I froze up, knowing I couldn't stay here, and the fact that he remembered me.

"Yes, I am."

"Yeah, I remember Howard," he said, "good dude."

"I don't think I want to see any more, drive me over to the post office."

"Which one?" he asked, puzzled by the request.

"Well, you know what, just let me out," I said to him as I pulled cash from a pocket, handed it to him, and pounced from the back seat when he stopped. I looked to the sky, took a deep breath, and headed for Irwin Street walking fast, almost at a trot as I feared he would call someone and broadcast I was in town. I ducked behind a dumpster, ran through some woods, and came out a mile later in grandmama's backyard, though she had died twenty years ago, and another family lived there now. Seeing a father and son shooting hoops in the driveway I turned back and went past Ronnie's old house and heard some sirens go off. I ducked behind a car, looked for action, saw none and ran back down Irwin until I faced a policeman patrolling near the old 619 Club. Spooked, he came towards me, asked where I was going, then followed as I jolted over the bank near Ollie's service station. I picked up a rubber hose from the ground and hit him six times. He fell, tried to get out his weapon but I jumped to secure his arm and beat him about the head. Two men saw me and said nothing. I walked to a bus stop at the corner and boarded the next bus to Collier Heights. I sat, unsure as to what just happened, but I knew I should not have come back.

The piece of paper on the bench was a twenty-dollar bill rolled into itself. My heart raced, and I slipped it into my pants pocket unsure of this brand of luck. I feared someone would come back and ask for it. As I pushed over to the window side seat, I tried not to look worried as I searched faces to see if anyone noticed what I had just discovered. I thought to get off at the next stop as I figured the cop had relayed to his precinct what had happened and given a description of his attacker. I got off, saw I was near Tyler Park, and hurried down the hill to the pavilion. I saw a few guys milling about the bar-b-que pit, so I went over there. I didn't recognize anyone and simply said hello and kept moving on to the tennis courts nearby. The feeder railroad track was just beyond, and I crossed over the tracks to Larkin Street, which used to be a bad area, but was amazed how it was cleaned up with large homes and manicured lawns. This was interesting and I felt stumped until a car pulled up and the driver side window was lowered, and a voice spoke, "Ms. Charlotte, what's up girl? Where you been?" I stared at him, and it was Tanya's older brother, Donald Gaines, we were not friends but knew each other from back in the days of drug use.

"Hey, what's up?" I say to him.

"Just chilling, where you headed?" he asked.

"I'm not sure. I'm just back, and you know, trying to stay up."

"That's it, stay up! All right, I'm going to pull. I'll see you around."

"Yeah, I'll be around. I'll see you."

He rolled up his window and slowly drove away. I could see him raise his phone up to his ear, probably to call Tanya.

I looked around at the houses and wondered who lived here now. This was a complete flip from thirty years ago. I figured I better move on, but before I could decide, I hear a strong voice speak from a house off to my left about thirty-five yards away, "Charlotte, Charlotte Rainey, over here, It's William, William Brown, what's up?" He waved his arms rolling inward for me to come over to the house. I looked around and headed that way.

William was an old friend as well who had worked as a demolition contractor for realtors. He would go in and break a house down to the basics, sell the scrap, recycle carpets and the like, take usable items to a salvage store, and generally clear out the place according to what was asked. His small company was viable for over thirty years and afforded a good family life for him, his wife, and their three kids. He employed three to seven people at a time and worked year-round, taking off for holidays and two-week long vacations a year. He was a blessed guy and stayed away from the streets.

Walking up to the house I felt proud for him and a bit wistful for myself, William was someone I could talk to, and I needed to sort out my next moves.

"Hey Charlotte, so good to see you, brother Gaines called and said you were in the area. Come in, let's catch up," he offered.

"Thanks William, so kind of you, I'm in a bit of a pickle," I say up front.

"No worries let's see what you got, and we'll handle it. Have a seat over here," he gestures to a chair by a window in the living room. His wife Mary comes in and says to me, "Charlotte, good to see you after all these years!"

I stand, and she comes over to give me a hug.

"Would you like something to eat or drink?" she asks.

"I would, a sandwich, some juice with water if you have it."

"Sure, make yourself comfortable and I'll bring it out in a few."

"Thank you," I respond.

"So," William starts out, "we know about the past, what's up now?"

"Well, I just got out of prison, and it's been trouble ever since. Can I talk freely?"

"Sure, no one else is here. We can go in the den if you like, close the door, Mary will understand."

"No, this is good. It may take me a minute to share the whole story."

"That's fine, I'm retired now, take your time."

"Okay, thanks. You remember Lorna, don't you? She helped me during the last few years of my bid. Well, that was a mistake. She had me do something when I got out, you know, a deal with her stepbrother Harvey that didn't go down as planned and some people got hurt."

"That wasn't you was it, those two dudes over on Irwin Street last week?"

"Okay, okay, let me tell you what happened. I was there, but it wasn't me."

We both settle in our chairs before Mary brings in the food. I figured I could get honest with William; he had done some work for Howard in the past, and we had a good long history, and the truth might help keep me free.

After my talk with William I checked into the hospital for treatment in the post- traumatic stress disorder program for veterans of the war on drugs. I was there two months. That's when I found out Howard was still alive but using an alias. Be careful!

Charlotte Rainey

"That's pretty interesting," was all Charlie said at first.

"It is interesting that she put that on paper. What do you think she wanted me to know, or do?"

"Man, I don't have a clue," Charlie says in response. "Tell me something, I haven't seen you in over thirty something years and you wind up on my doorstep with this. Yeah, we did some things, but you know I was not in the streets that long. I was a guest. What are you looking for from me?" Charlie asks.

"You're one of the only people from back then still living I feel I can trust."

"Wait a minute now, Don, I'm retired and run a little restaurant here near the beach. My work the last twenty-eight years was nice and neat. Not too complicated. Regina and I have a simple life. I'm too old for this kind of drama, and you should be let sleeping dogs lie!"

"You're right, I'm sorry I came your way with this," Don says.

"Were they really brother and sister?" Charles asks Don.

"They, well, they were close. I don't know if it was true," Don offers.

"Yeah, but things happened. Look let's get a snack and go to the beach. We can talk out there," Charlie suggests.

*

Tyler Johnson arrived in Darian about eleven o'clock on Tuesday. He had checked in to a hotel not far from the diner. As a matter of fact, he watched Charles and Don walk the narrow street to the beach entrance sixty yards away. He thought they looked chummy carrying provisions and the large umbrella to camp out for a spell on the beach. Two old guys with little else to do though Charles did have the diner to keep him occupied. Don, however, did look to be in good shape still, ever the athlete, he probably still worked out. Tyler thought he'd rest awhile, maybe join them on the beach or for a cocktail later somewhere. He was in no hurry. Accounts would be settled.

*

Darian was a small town just south of Shady Dale, maybe twenty miles. It was populated mostly by older residents who had grown up there and had not seen a reason to leave. There was just enough government and general commercial work to sustain a good living, and with the tourist trade, and retirees who had discovered its charm there was enough activity to keep the shops, grocers, small art museums, and theater alive. It was a beach town with the smells of casual comfort for the roughly nine thousand inhabitants.

The marshes were green and lush this year for May helped by steady rain in March and slightly above average temperatures all year. The breezes were pleasant and though a couple of storms in early in the month raised concern shorts, tees, and soft shoes remained the attire of choice.

Charles chose a spot just away from a sand bar and backed by a dune just up from the public entrance to the beach. They set up their chairs and the umbrella after digging the eight-inch-deep hole with the screw in plastic base holder. It was a pleasant time of day, low tide, and not many people out walking or lounging about the clean, white sands. The air was calm and the few pelicans and cranes that flew over didn't squawk to announce their presence. Good conversation could be had here now. After sitting they both bit into their sandwiches and Don starts the review.

"September 4, 1989, apartments over on Larkin me, you, and Howard after Freddie's was robbed and we got the numbers' money, eight thousand, all that dope we shot. Two weeks later Milkman was killed, well, overdosed on a bad batch of drugs. Remember we didn't see Howard for a month after that. Remember how we got busted over at Charlotte's house a week later. Who set that up?"

"Man, I forgot about that. Well, I remember getting busted and the robbery, but I forgot about Milk," Charlie says.

"Where I'm going is that was Howard's dope. He killed that boy because he was tapping Charlotte and Howard didn't like that. So, was she Howard's sister or old lady?"

"See, I don't remember all that."

"Okay. You weren't in the streets like that. Okay. But you do remember whose dope we were getting back then, right?" Don asks.

"Hold up. Help me out here, why are we talking about this?" Charlie asks. "If he's still alive he may be coming after me because he thinks I know about that and the stuff with Charlotte and Lorna."

"But that was later, right?" Don says. "Just think Charlotte for a moment. Why was she so screwed?"

"Jail time and the street life, drugs. All that!" Charlie says.

"True, but Howard had a hold on her, used to knock her around sometimes. She was a social worker before she got so bad off you know."

"I didn't know that."

"What I'm saying is if Howard's coming after you, he's coming after me too because he thinks I know what you know."

"And what do you know?" Charlie slides in.

"I can't tell you."

"Then why are we out here talking?"

"Just in case."

Tyler had been on the 'crazy' pills for about a year. The undertaker who had helped with the deception had died of natural causes, and Tyler had not been exposed. His physical features had changed a bit from exercising his jaw in a deformed way, and the glasses he wore were usually halfcocked over his eyes and just barely hanging on to his ears. He seemed in another world when approached so most left him alone while he lived on Oliver Street. What people found out was he went to the mental health clinic once a week but still looked 'bugged out' as it were. His speech was cryptic, and he slobbered sometimes and let it drip to his shirt or jacket. Every once and a while he would go to a spot and drink alcohol with the fellows, or smoke weed in the park, but he didn't talk much just smiled and looked kind of odd. It was a good act, and he slowly returned to normalcy over the six months before moving to the retirement village stopping the medication, living in another part of the city, and taking on the persona of someone recovering from trauma who was being professionally withdrawn off the meds with some physical reconstruction of the facial muscles. The apartment manager at Oliver's Crossing was amazed the day Tyler brought the keys in and let them know he was moving out, as the well dressed and slick moving, hand gesturing Tyler said as he entered the office, "What's up player?" looking nothing like the 'crazy' man who had leased the apartment fourteen months ago.

*

For about thirty years their lives were all similar. Businesspeople, not too outspoken, well liked with good people skills, although Howard still peddled drugs and dealt with thieves. Don and Charles presented as basic, good dudes while Howard was always a smoothie. Their connections and actions from the past were history. Howard kept accounts however and when Charlotte was squeezed by the cold case detectives to give them names about several murders his came up. Charlotte did confide in him and that's when Howard started his ruse.

*

Larkin Street had been one of the most notorious drug streets in Shady Dale, but that's where the best drugs were, and Howard controlled the market. Charlotte had placed Howard at the scene with motives to kill Chuck and Larry. They had stolen from him and got what was coming. Sonny Jones had taken the fall for Howard and some money was passed on to his family. Now, Tyler wanted to clarify with Don that everything was okay from long ago, about Milk, if that was why Don had reached out with his posts on social media. Don was glad that he had not heard back from Howard since receiving the letter from Charlotte. Certain secrets were about to be exposed, and he needed to be careful.

*

Part of the difficulty for people who had periods of heavy drug and or alcohol use is that participation in certain events or living experiences was not put into the memory bank properly. Things were done with no recollection soon after, or many years later. Such was the case with Charles now as much of what Don was describing was lost on him.

"I just remember Larkin Street was a bad place and we went there maybe two times," Charles said.

"No, it was more like ten and you decided it was time to give up the drugs because it was too uncomfortable over there," Don says to him.

"Man, it was way out of my zip code! I know you grew up over there, but it was a scary place."

"I know, but anyway do you remember Milkman?"

"No, I don't."

"So, you don't remember what happened to him?"

"No. You know, I was not hard core. That was what, a year and a half of my life, the time running the streets with you, then eight months in county. That's all. You mentioned Howard Taylor, I just remember him, and that broad Charlotte sold the dope, and when we made that money, we spent time with them. I never felt connected to the lifestyle."

"Did you ever bang her?" Don asks trying to jog his memory.

"If I did, I don't remember," Charles says. "Look, when we were out that night, early morning really, and we went our separate ways I left all that behind never to address it again. When daddy came and got me out of jail, I said to myself that was it. And I told him. I really hadn't thought about those times much since."

"So, if I said you had killed somebody during that time you don't remember?"

"That's pretty absurd, I think I would remember that!"

"Okay, good."

About this time the man with the crooked face was standing a few feet away waving to get their attention to ask a question.

"Howdy friends, how y'all doing?" he said.

"Hey, good, how are you doing?" Don said and Charles waved.

"I'm good, look, this is my first time on a beach, and I wanted some information," he says.

"Sure, come on over, let's talk. My name is Don, and this is Charles."

"Okay. My name is Tyler. Good to meet you two guys."

Chapter 2

The man in the wheelchair with the dog and his wife noticed Tyler Johnson as he came out of his room on the second floor of the hotel. His facial disfiguration seemed forced, not from an injury or disease. They gave a soft greeting and processed their thoughts later. The man, Horace Stinson, had been a detective on the case of Harold Watkins, the funeral director who had helped Howard with the deception. His forensic training had led him to further investigate Mr. Watkins's death of natural causes at the age of fifty-three, and that led him to the assassination of Mr. Taylor shortly thereafter. Horace had done some special effects work with a film production company before getting into law enforcement and some of this seemed staged. His research on the two bodies before and after Mr. Taylor showed some documentation errors that supported a notion that something was not correct. When he scanned the man's face in the hallway a twinge of discomfort tickled his brain cells. A puzzle piece fell into place with a jolt, and he made a phone call back up to Atlanta.

"Yeah, I'm pretty sure that's him," Horace said to the officer in charge of cases under ten years old. "Check the last addendum from my report of August 23, 2015. It's a hand-written note."

"Okay, I'll do it. Thanks Horace. How's retirement?"

"Not good; you see I'm still working!" They both laugh.

"It's just been a year, maybe you'll come back?" David Thompson asks him.

"Maybe, the juices are flowing again."

"Okay, take care. I'll get back to you."

Don gets a call from his wife Arleen saying someone had broken into their rental. He excuses himself to rush there and Charles and Tyler continue the conversation.

"So how about women. We're about the same age, how does it work?" Tyler was asking.

"You're on your own there. I'm married so it's just friendships. Most of the people down here are not too complicated, usually old friends. The beach is a place to relax, let the world go by. It's according to what you're looking for, especially at this stage of the game, everybody's been around the block a time or two by now," Charlie smiles and they booth laugh.

"Yeah, yeah, I never married. I'm here as a stop on a journey to try new things. I've always had a friend or two, but nothing serious. I moved into a retirement home about a year ago and it's good. Good people. Good activities. People are friendly," Tyler shares. "How about you and your friend?"

"I live here, he's here to get some sun and move on. We were just talking over old times."

"I guess this is a good place to do that?" Tyler says, looking around taking in the view, listening to the waves, watching the kids and family members playing games or coming back and forth from the water to their camps.

"So, what's been your life's work?" Charles asks the stranger.

'Investor,' simple, money man. No kids, like I said no wives, no long-term relationships."

"Good, I have a small diner in the village. I did standard office work for years. Money man too, procurements."

"Guard the money!"

"Yep."

Tyler started to ask a few more questions but decided this was enough for today.

"Okay, well good. Thanks for talking to me. I'll see you around. What's the name of your place?"

"Harry's Diner. My father's name," Charles shares.

"Okay I'll have to get by there at some point. I'm here for a week. Probably go up to Savannah to visit some friends while I'm down this way."

"Okay, good. Take care."

They say good-byes and Charles calls home.

"Regina, hey babe. What's happening?" Charles asks.

"Quiet here. I was napping. Are you at work?" she asks.

"No, I'm leaving the beach. I was here with my old acquaintance Don who came by the diner. He and his wife are on their way to New Mexico. They're just here for a few days."

"Refresh my memory?"

"You don't know him. We go back to the drug days. I've probably mentioned him a few times over the years."

"I guess. You don't talk about that much."

"Yeah. Not worth talking about."

"What did y'all talk about?" she asks him.

"You know small talk, what we've done since. We haven't seen each other in over thirty-five years. More than that really, we were young."

"Okay, are you coming home?"

"Yep. I'll call the shop and get a report on how things are going. Oh, Don did have to leave early because someone broke into the house they are renting. I guess he'll let me know what happened. Maybe not."

"Oh wow, too bad."

"Okay, bye."

"Bye."

Driving across the causeway and heading to the north end of the island where they lived Charles smiled and laughed to himself as he recalled the times he spent with Charlotte. They had made love on several occasions and professed a desire to be together as a couple. Charlotte, three years younger was lean and willowy with smooth skin and luscious lips. Her body form was poetic and taut, her hair was long and suggestive of play time, her chest sloped like a summer hill rolling to the west following the pull of the sun. Charles, athletic and strong was three inches taller and could carry her around the room body bottom up, full insertion, with a complete embrace. They would sweat and moan, scratch and pull, craving an intimacy from books that lie, yet there they were totally involved romantic nourishment wild and free.

His return to reality was abrupt when his phone rang and it was the diner relaying a message from Don that all was well and it was probably teenagers who rambled around a bit in the house but because of the large, solid safe provided their few valuables were not compromised. Still, they decided to leave the island later that night and that he would call back at some point.

Charles pulled into his driveway disturbed by today's events. These were people and experiences he'd all but forgotten were part of his story. After discharging from the military, he had kicked around a bit with several jobs and girlfriends and hung out with guys who were restless and searching as well. He had met Don on a temporary job assignment in a warehouse up in Atlanta over on Ponce de Leon Circle and they had gone to a few baseball games together on double dates. The girls had been nice and friendly, though already on career paths in professional jobs. Drinking was light and a little pot was smoked but it was not the main ingredient of their outings. All was cool until one day after work Don asked if Charles wanted to try something a stronger. Being both naïve and curious he said yes, and they snorted some heroin. It was instant love for Charles and within days he wanted to inject the substance. They did and a month later they left the job and were hanging in the streets getting high and stealing to supply what had become a drug habit in short order. Handy and skillful Charles enjoyed the challenges of each day until things got rough when someone tried to rob them, and Don almost killed the guy and took his knife. That was followed by a series of thefts, some drug dealing and hooking up with Howard Taylor to go down south to explore some other opportunities to make money. Howard's dealings were on another level where violence was expected as a part of business dealings for drugs and commodities. The night Charles passed out in a small apartment on

Larkin and saw a well-dressed Charlotte performing oral sex on three guys was too stimulating. He was aroused in a new way and pursued her when she came around for drugs the next week. Little did he know her connection to Howard and that making out with her would put his life in danger. Two days after he and Don robbed the convenience store is when Charles was compromised, and he had to commit a crime that he was just now remembering. This all was becoming too real and when he was arrested and sent to county jail, he was somewhat relieved.

Regina met him in the driveway with a warm smile and embrace. She was old school southern charm with sharp facial features on her round contoured face. He smiled as well but she could tell he was not quite right.

"How are you darling?" she asked, grabbing his hand, and walking him to the side of the house towards the floral garden.

"You know that guy I told you about, Don, the old acquaintance, well he brought up stuff that I'd rather forgotten about. Stuff that happened before we met. I guess I should tell you about it," he said to her.

"Let's sit over here in the shade," she guided him to a bench under an oak tree.

"Sure, I probably need to go to the restroom first," he tells her.

"Okay, something to drink?" she asks.

"Yeah, iced tea probably. I guess I could use a piece of cake too."

"Okay, I'll meet you back out here."

After talking with his wife Charles became moody and withdrawn. He didn't give her too much detail but just enough information for her to also withdraw somewhat. Theirs was a good marriage of twenty-seven years and this would be another brick in the wall as it were to solidify their union. Fear, regret, confusion, and prayer would be a part of the household until Charles could recall more details and get some answers. Little did he know that the stranger Tyler would become the source of truth and danger.

Chapter 3

Howard's mother had a diagnosed mental illness. There was a kitchen fire that killed her husband, and she moved back in with her parents to help raise an eight years old Howard and his brother Philip who was twelve. She was unable to work and didn't speak much. She was a beautiful woman but was lost in another world somewhere after the accident.

Both boys were industrious and found ways to earn money after school when not out playing around with their friends. When he got older Philip worked for a small night club in the neighborhood washing dishes and cleaning up the lounge a few evenings a week. The owner took a liking to him, perhaps too much so at times, and after high school he moved away. Howard would pick up change in various ways, but his primary interest was in sports betting. He remembered player and team statistics, histories and such and used that information to get an edge. School seemed boring, though he passed all his classes, and when he graduated, he joined the Army, performed well, and discharged honorably after six years. He had been a quartermaster and earned extra making sure everything was starched and tight and troops had the provisions they needed. He shined shoes, kept brass buckles bright, and was the go-to man to be in tip top shape for inspections and training exercises. He was perfect in close order drills and loved the precise, regimented movements necessary for ceremony. The brothers did not stay in touch and knew very little how well each was doing in their chosen fields of work and lifestyle.

The water filling the basin sounded loud and fresh as Don prepared to shave and get ready to drive the mile and a half to the small airport. Their flight was for seven and they would arrive in Albuquerque about seven forty. Arleen was packed and ready and didn't seem too disturbed by the intrusion on their beach plans. Don, however, was anxious and sweaty, not sure if he could trust Charles now that they had talked. The eyes always suggest when someone is lying, and Charles had trouble maintaining eye contact as they talked on the beach. Those days were rough and lively times, and Charles loved every minute of it! He was a dope fiend of the highest order and relished the power of carrying pistols and taking money. Don was sure he remembered the gunfight over on La France Street and his cool answer, "I don't know if I killed him or not," was his response the next day when they processed the robbery of Freddie's Market and being chased to there. It had been an eight-thousand-dollar lick, and they had shopped and partied with the Bryant twin sisters afterwards. The desert air would help him recall a few more details on what happened and what he would need to do to stay alert.

"Horace, it's David Thompson. How are you?"

"Good, good, what'd you find out?"

"You may have been on to something. Watkins owed Howard Taylor a lot of money, about sixty-grand. It was money Mr. Watkins had gambled away and he was about to lose the funeral home due to some unpaid taxes," David tells him. Taylor had been implicated in two murders and was about to be locked up when he was 'killed' at that wedding over on Beckwith. This is where it gets strange, your report, the original was not in the files, it was a copy. Plus, the death certificates for two men had been 'altered' and the one for Mr. Taylor had to be refiled. His was a closed casket affair; you see where this is going."

"I do. Watkins."

"Heart attack, right!"

"Oh, I remember now, family history, blah, blah."

"Yeah, too young."

"Okay, thanks. I'll be back in Atlanta in a week. Meanwhile I'm going to try and engage this guy down here. I might get lucky."

*

Growing up Howard and Philip loved to play make believe games where each would become someone else and act out a scene from a movie. Howard liked Eddie G. Robinson and would do the neck and tight voice thing as he pretended to face other gangsters. Philip liked the more intellectual roles played by Gary Cooper especially the high noon scene. He'd put on one of his grandfather's hats, a badge he had saved from a toy pistol set and would strain his eyes to show the fear yet resolve and recite those lines about duty. After a few rounds of speaking parts, they would laugh and promise that one day they would be great actors and make a lot of money.

Charlotte was drunk and smelled of multiple sex acts the morning she walked off her only real job. She worked for a social services unit of the state department of health. She had broken just about every ethical code you could name regarding peer relations. She was often late for work, slept with her boss and a co-worker on occasion, had stolen money from the office, and missed work assignments repeatedly. It took HR two months to compile the list of infringements, document corroboration, and finally interview her and state how tenuous her future employment had become. The morning she walked off the job she had been out most of the night, tried cocaine for the first time, and had drank probably a fifth of vodka. She was just twenty-two years old and had only been out of college nine months. She met Howard Taylor at the Pay Day Loan office he owned.

"I'll have to let you speak to the owner," the frustrated clerk told her when she refused to increase her debt limit, and Charlotte had become verbally abusive.

"Yes, miss, how may I help?" he spoke coming from behind the counter to face her.

"You see I need some money until my bonus comes. I make good money so just give me a new limit. You know I'm a good customer by my records. That old broad over there could have done it she knows me. And who are you?" she asked him.

"I'm Mr. Taylor, the owner," he told her.

"Okay, good, you can give me the money, eight-fifty, that's all. I'll just pay it all next time; you know the twelve hundred already on the books. You can do that can't you Mr. good looking. So, what's up anyway?"

"Miss, your name is Charlotte Rainey, right?" he says to her. "We can't confirm your employment status. Were you recently fired?"

"Look, is that any of your business, you just want your money, right, plus interest, you don't care how I get it do you, mister?" she says as seductively as she can under her present state of substance impairment. "We can work it out, you know, handsome. You sure do have a fine body, what's up?" she repeats.

"Miss Rainey we can't do anything else, sorry," he says to her, becoming slightly aroused as she moves around the office. "Just be sure to make your payment next week," he says to her and winks not allowing his staff person to see his move.

"Okay darling, I'll do that. Next week, Tuesday it's due, right?" she looks over at the clerk.

"Yes ma'am, Tuesday, eighty-four dollars."

"Okay, next Tuesday about ten o'clock I'll be here with the money," speaking in a more conciliatory tone, signaling to Howard if he was game.

"Thank you, Miss Rainey, have a good day," Howard says to her.

"You too sugar, have a good day."

She leaves the premises, tired, and ready for some serious sleep. Howard watches her walk out the door and into the parking lot. He can still feel that rush of chemical attraction fueled by Charlotte's alcohol altered body movements.

*

The four months Don was in the county lockup for loitering he had met a guy who was a wholesale marijuana trader named Keith Balam and when Don got his courier service going Keith approached him to move some product for him. Being early in recovery and needing some cash flow Don delivered a few pounds a week for a couple of months then decided it was too risky and stopped. Keith understood and no more was made of the relationship. With hard work, luck, and a desire to build a new life Don cultivated contacts and within a year had enough regular clients to support himself. The business was moving forward, and he met Arleen at a small business leadership conference. They exchanged numbers, became friendly, and she tossed some good business contacts his way. She was distribution manager for a local art supplies company which had revenues of a little over a million a year retail and Don's courier service became provider of choice for their deliveries. They dated for a year and married in a small chamber service with the judge and three couples they knew as participants. The reception was held in a coffee shop across the street from the courthouse and they all had pie and drinks and lots of laughter.

Chapter 4

Miss Charlotte Rainey arrived at the loan office the following Tuesday at nine-fifty-five and Howard was waiting for her at pay window number 3. She was dressed modestly, brown slacks, a white ruffled blouse open just enough to show some cleavage, and flats. Her appearance and carriage were calm as she seemed sober and rested. Howard greeted her warmly and waved her up to the window as no other customers were sitting in the lobby waiting. She smiled at him and approached and offered a firm good morning.

"Thank you," Howard spoke, "good morning to you too."

"It's a good day, I'm blessed," she said.

Howard was thinking how different she looked today compared to last week, not the same fluid movements, and certainly the voice was non-threatening this time.

"So, how may I help you today?" he asks her.

"Well I'm here to pay on my loan." She reaches into her handbag and retrieves six one hundred bills and gives them to him. He takes the money, counts it, looks over past leger entries and writes in today's payment. He gives her a receipt with the updated balance and asks if there's anything else he can do for her. She says no and walks out saying, "Have a nice day." He responds with, "You too."

Charlotte found a job through a temporary agency doing clerical work for a shipping company in a heavy industrial area northwest of the city. It was a gritty section prominent with low rent hotels, huge warehousing facilities, truck stops, gas stations, and any manor of human vice products. There was lots of foot traffic as workers and street people moved about to the various businesses that served the almost endless supply of trucks and heavy labor jobs abundant in the area. Mountains of pallets, trucks tied tight with large plates of unfinished slabs of granite, and sixteen wheelers moving up and down the busy corridor hauling all manner of goods, legal or otherwise, that populated the noisy, visual atmosphere. It was a rough area for rough people, and it was the city's largest tax base. Major state and interstate roads intersected nearby to keep everything humming with not too much backup or oversight.

*

Oscar 'Milkman' Cleveland was one of those rough customers. He was tall, well-built, and talked gently but looked like a thug with his strong jawbone, dark eyes, and deep-set forehead. His eyes were a bit too intimidating though he was someone you wanted to like but there was an aura of some hidden agenda as you talked to him. It was not a fear, but a disease that put one on guard. He spent time at the Second Oasis Hotel on the main strip of Brown Industrial Boulevard selling women and promises. He was a hustler and player, heroin addict, and had a reputation for taking money, and being lucky yet unlucky. The summer of 1978 he hit a lottery jackpot for forty-two thousand dollars and a week later happened by a money transfer truck where a bag with twenty-six thousand dollars was sitting on the sidewalk in front of a bank that had slipped off the hand truck used by the armored car's security guard and Milk had picked it up and smoothly kept walking folding it under his shirt. He was seen by two guys who didn't like him, and they tipped the police to where he could be found. The marshals picked him up a week later and he was tried, convicted, and sent to prison for ten years. When he got out, he stayed good about a month then was up to his old tricks, even stealing two eight balls of cocaine from one of Howard's runners. Two weeks later he bought some dope over on Larkin and was given a 'hot shot' and died in the basement of his mother's house in East Point. No one was charged with an offense, and Don and Charlie never spoke of what they knew.

*

Howard owned several of the small apartment homes on both sides of the street on Larkin. He had been given two by his granddaddy and he bought four more as they became available. He also owned a small used car dealership, the payday loan company, and kept two hand car wash enterprises going run by a couple of neighborhood guys who had done serious fed time and didn't want to do any other kind of work. Howard was fair with the people who worked for him, especially the knuckleheads who ran the dope traffic. By the age of forty he was considered a kingpin and seemed to walk on water. Things would get a little tricky when Charlotte came to work for him, by then a full-fledged dope fiend and street person who had Howard wrapped around her fingers. No one could talk to him the way she did, nor would he bail people out of jail as often as he did for her. She was a total mess, but he stuck by her. When those 'college boys' Don and Charles started hanging around that's when Howard's mood swings became more pronounced, and he would threaten people and hurt people in unnecessary ways if they fooled around with her. He had even pushed Milk down a flight of stairs once and said he'd kill Charles if he got too close to Charlotte. That didn't stop Charlotte and Charles from getting together a few times on the sly. Don, for his part, feared Charlotte and moved away from her when she would come into the shooting gallery and beg for drugs. He didn't like her and didn't want to risk the leads Howard would throw their way for potential robbery targets. Don would get good and high but maintain some sense of place and what was going on around him, but Charles would nod off and miss things, game slippage, they called it. That's why he had trouble remembering what he'd done once to save Charlotte's life. He was in a blackout and acted on instinct. Don had given him the pistol, then disposed of it. The police found the body in the park over on Oliver Street the next morning. Charlotte, twisted in thought about the whole matter had accused Don of acting like her older brother which brought up the question of parentage and as the conversation became more heated

Charlotte schooled Don about their father, the facts of which Howard had discovered and shared with Charlotte. Don's father David had strayed with Charlotte's mother Holly Robinson right before he was killed in the fire. Charlotte was four years younger than Don.

Chapter 5

Harold Watkins was sweaty and nervous about today's third service. It was for Howard Taylor. Hundreds had come to the funeral home to pay their respects by walking to the closed casket, stopping to offer a prayer or a thank you, and otherwise reflecting upon some instance of goodness done for them by the man. He had not been some kind of pest or hero in the community. He ran good businesses that helped people so most could overlook the drug dealing as it seemed a quiet personal affair.

Harold fixed and dressed the body appropriately but feared getting exposed by some freak accident and the stand in being discovered. His heart pounded in his chest, and he had to keep wiping the moisture from his brow with an almost endless supply of white handkerchiefs. He had felt faint several times and thought he would pass out before the end of the service at Shady Dale Cemetery. It went off without a hitch, however, and Mr. Harold Taylor was given a proper sendoff, supposedly.

*

Horace Stinson was disappointed after leaving the funeral because this would close the case of the murders over on Larkin and that of Milkman. All the evidence pointed to Howard Taylor and the DA had been ready to present it to the grand jury and issue an indictment. All through the service Stinson had felt something was not right and mentioned that in his final report, and that he would file an addendum if new information was discovered.

As coroner for the county seat of Rutledge Watkins was able to confirm the cause of death and identify the bodies. In his dual role it was easy for him to manipulate the certifications. His own death occurred from the stress of what he had done and conversations he had with Horace Stinson about discrepancies with some of the paperwork confirming the disposition of Howard Taylor's body just after the gunshots caused guests at the wedding to run for cover and scatter all over the church lot. As the initial investigations progressed Watkins identified the body as Howard Taylor, sealed the body bag, and filed his reports with the police department.

Horace Stinson had been a detective for eighteen years and the Howard Taylor case was to be his last before he retired. His injury had occurred while chasing a couple of bums down Burbank Street while investigating Howard's drug dealing operation and the Larkin Street murders. He had slipped and rolled over down a hill and sprained his right ankle badly and broke his left leg below the calf. The nature of his injuries required extensive rehabilitation and a year later he still had to use a wheelchair on occasions when he had long walks to get from place to place. The morning he saw Tyler Johnson he and his wife had finished a swim in the hotel's pool and a short walk on the beach. He had over done it, and the beach safety patrol had to wheel them around to the hotel lobby in the back of a four-wheeler and had provided the wheelchair for him to use.

*

As Howard became Tyler, he had gained weight and lost it, developed a full body exercise regimen, took notes, and had a facial reconstruction specialist teach him how to alter the contours of his face by way of myofascial massage to establish new muscle memory. He would sit for hours near the county mental health clinic and observe clients come and go, taking notes on gait, gestures, and types of glasses they wore paying attention to how they set them on their faces. He was able to purchase Risperdal and Zyprexa, anti-psychotic drugs, from the brother of a friend who had stopped taking his prescriptions to get used to the effects of the medications. He would take to purposely scramble his brain to make more authentic his presentation as possibly schizophrenic. He even had a worker go with him as his guardian to secure his apartment and on several visits to the doctor. After being diagnosed he performed around town for over two months to establish community presence and history, and all necessary paperwork was completed. His new identity secured Tyler Johnson was viable.

Chapter 6

Don usually felt very relaxed in New Mexico. The surroundings, the air, the views gave him a peace of mind he could not feel back home. Now he had an urgency about feeling relaxed as he thought of Howard Taylor still being alive. Charlotte's letter had awakened his recall of events that had been placed in the memory vault almost forty years ago. Bad things had happened because of his relationship with Howard Taylor and Charles Riley. Four people knew the exact level of Howard's treachery, one was dead, and one had claimed memory loss. He felt he was on his own, yet he would need to talk with Charlie some more to make sure they were on solid ground. Charlie could have been lying about what he remembered. And if Howard were still alive and the authorities got wind of that fact would Howard turn on him?

"Are we going over to the art district first?" Arleen had called out to him, bringing him back to the present.

"Yes, I'd rather do that today and drive up to Taos tomorrow," Don responded feeling like he had been freed from a mental bondage. He had thought of little else since Arleen called about the break-in. He didn't remember much about the flight, checking into the hotel, or making love with her earlier that morning. Survival, animalistic instincts had taken over.

Larry Fleming received a phone call from Dr. Derick Scott, medical director for the addictive disease unit of Avery Mental Institute.

"This is Larry Fleming; how may I help you?" Larry answered.

"Mr. Fleming this is Dr. Derick Scott, how are you today?"

"I'm good, thanks."

"The reason for my call is that we would like for you to renew your group sessions. We were pleased with the work you had done in helping clients with post-traumatic stress disorder related to addiction, and thus recovery over the life span of the addict. Now, we are particularly interested in treating the criminal aspects and how that impedes a full recovery. We are curious how the addict can realistically blot out terrible crimes, not have a sense of moral or legal responsibility, and continue to live a normal life. We would like to know the psychology involved. Curiously, some major brains have reviewed some of your clinical notes and your use of poetry to create an intimate setting to achieve said goals and are very impressed with your results. What we haven't resolved for this study is that some of our new clients are linked to murders and other crimes and we likely will have to cross some boundaries."

"I understand," Larry responds.

"We have full histories done by our staff psychiatrists..." the doctor pauses and Larry comments.

"They question the validity of my credentials, not my long history of working in this area already."

"Exactly."

"Will I have to work with them?" Larry asks.

"Yes, they will review the clinicals with you and sit in on groups on occasion. There should be two therapists in the group anyway, as you well know," the doctor clarifies. "But they all know of your work and reputation. They are pleased to get a chance to work with you. You are a legend you know."

"Thanks, yes. When do we start?"

"Can you be at the hospital today at noon, my office?"

"Yes sir, I can be there."

Chapter 7

The last two months Larry had been feeling better, his grieving over Darlene's death, two years now, was less intense, and he was enjoying semi-retirement. He was sleeping longer and more restfully each night, his weight was steady at 198 pounds, and he was playing golf again. He had a couple of casual dates last month, but not much to speak of as he was not interested in investing too much time to anyone. He was not isolating as he had begun to attend twelve step meetings again after not going for twenty years. They had helped when he first got clean and sober but eventually, he stopped going. Things had gone well, his life was full and busy, his marriage to Darlene had been great, but ever since he cut back on work a few years ago some old instincts had kicked back in, and with that call to his brother Leroy and the threats that were made, then Darlene's death, he had gotten to a very dark place and was planning to harm the instigator. Following the man from the hospital that day was a wake-up call as Larry was going to extinguish the one person who could connect him to the bombing all those years ago. The call from Dr. Scott was a God send and he was ready to return to higher principles. Once more he could use his experiences to help others.

*

The worktable in Dr. Scott's office was a beautiful honey wood oak one hundred years old. It was rounded at the ends and seventy-one by forty-three inches. There were small black spots about the surface and some discoloration, but mainly it was well preserved and durable to withstand movements of paper chart folders without metal clips atop. And now that most charting was electronic doctor had positioned a quarter inch pad to protect the tabletop from phones, tablets, keys, and laptops being placed upon it.

Present for the meeting were MDs Assam and Dunlap, psychologist Heard, and Dr. Scott, MD. Everyone stood and clapped when Larry Fleming entered the room, offering well-earned respect and appreciation for his body of work the past thirty years. He was taken aback and nodded gently to the assembled and shook each ones' hand firmly, befitting his old school upbringing.

"Thank you," Larry says as he shares eye contact.

"Thank you for joining us on such short notice," Dr. Scott begins. "We are anxious to get started on what will be an important step in the treatment of PTSD Addiction Type."

"I am humbled by your belief in my past work and hope to make improvements with the help of all parties involved here, as well auxiliary staff persons. Will the clients be housed inpatient?" Larry asked, getting somewhat ahead of the proceedings.

"No. They will remain outpatient unless some crisis develops and there's a loss of control, or the associations become too intense for processing at the end of the hour and a half group session. A patient may need to stay afterwards to talk with a core member. Of course, we are the core clinicians and will be assigned patients to track," Dr. Scott presents.

"Legalities?" Larry presents.

"Confidentiality applies, but we must have ethical considerations in place. The histories so far allude to actions that are primarily over thirty years old, so that's one sub-set, the other is anything within the past five years, that could present some real problems," Dr. Scott shares.

"So, we won't know until we know?"

"Correct."

"Okay, first client," Larry asks.

Chapter 8

Both Don and Charles went missing two weeks before their participation in the group was to start. Arleen reported that Don had been drinking heavily ever since they returned home from New Mexico, and Regina found gas receipts from Shady Dale on Charles's laptop, as well as several unused diabetic syringes in shirt pockets on his side of the walk-in closet. Of course, Charles was not diabetic, and she did not want to believe that her seventy-three years old husband had returned to hard core drug use. They had contacted Dr. Scott who informed Larry and the team of the news. Along with this development two other registered participants had met with misfortune, Claudia Beasley a retired Bank examiner had committed suicide by a self-inflicted gunshot, and Eddie Anderson, an attorney had been arrested for aggravated bank fraud with no bond. Both had returned to substance abuse within the last few weeks. Contact had been made with Jefferey Hurston, Tyler Johnson, and Jennifer Tallant and they all were still planning to attend and were stable though both Jennifer and Jefferey had had an episode of relapse within the past month, and of course he had returned to his therapy group briefly six months ago then dropped out. Jennifer has been smoking marijuana off and on for the past sixty years. Tyler was riding out his new identity and was doing just fine if you can call his level of deception 'doing fine.' Unrehearsed both Charles and Don arrived in the Larkin Street area within a day of each other, both searching for drugs.

"It could be dangerous, but I feel I must try and find them," Larry responded to Dr. Scott's question about responsibility.

"Where would you start to look?"

"Based on their histories I think I have a good idea."

"Do you think they're together?"

"I don't know."

"You're the expert here."

"This is part of the process. What we know about their past dealings something spooked them."

"So how did they stay sturdy for so long?" doctor asked.

"Work, new lives, achievements."

"They're in their seventies why throw everything away now?" the doctor asked.

"It's why recovery is a life-long process; never cured! Something else has happened to them. That's what we're to find out."

"True."

Don arrived first and was walking around trying to get a sense of where the action was. He was dressed in jeans, a sports shirt, old sneakers, and a ball cap. The dope people had spotted him and didn't think he was a cop, too old. Or that he was looking for a lost grandchild who was smoking crack or hooked on opioids. No, this was someone who had been around and was after his own stuff. After a few passes it was determined that Nate would approach him.

"Hey old man, what's up?" Nate walked over to him.

"Hey guy, just out walking around. I used to know this area years ago," Don calmly responds.

"It's changed. I went away for a few years myself. What do you need?" Nate asked sensing this was someone who knew how to handle situations but was probably not armed.

"I don't know about you, but I used to shoot those narcotics. The good stuff used to be over here, but that was thirty years ago."

"It's still here."

"Are you the man, or is there someone else I can talk to?"

"I could be, but I know people."

"Look, I need two eight balls of coke, and a half load of heroin to start. Is that how it's going today?"

"Yeah, I understand that language. What else?"

"New syringes."

"Do you need a spot?"

"No, I've got a place nearby."

"Step over here, let's see what you got."

They walk to the side of a building and Don shows five hundred-dollar bills.

"Is this enough to get me started?" he asks Nate.

"I can work with that."

Don gives him the money.

"Are you going to stay here, or do you want me to bring it to you somewhere else?"

"I'll be in a white pick-up truck around the corner."

Nate's phone rings but he doesn't answer. He looks to Don and says, "Ten minutes."

Fifteen minutes later Nate taps on the passenger side window of the truck, and Don motions for him to get in.

"Here you go," Nate says as he gives Don the package. "Do you smoke crack, I forgot to ask?"

"No, no crack," Don answers as he inspects the goods by tasting the coke and smelling the heroin. He counts the six syringes and the cash change in the bag.

"Fresh cut and the best in the city," Nate shares.

"Here you go," Don says as he gives Nate a fifty-dollar bill from the change. "I may need more later."

"I don't think so brother, but I'll be around if you do. If I don't see you coming before midnight my brother Harold will be around. He'll be packing a pistol but don't trip. Wear what you got on now, so he'll know it's you."

"All right man, thanks."

Nate gets out of the truck and walks away; Don drives off slowly. He stops and pulls in behind one of the small buildings, pulls out his cap with water in it, cooks the heroin, shakes the coke in the syringe, draws up the heroin and pops the needle into an old injection site and has a true stick. He draws back blood, injects the drugs and in ten seconds feels as if he's about to throw up, then feels the exuberant rush, and tastes the coke smell. He goes up and smooths out, beginning a nod from long ago. Five minutes later he is alert enough to clean his works, put the everything bag in his jacket pocket and backs out the driveway heading east to his motel room twenty minutes away. Little did he know Charlie had already checked in to another property and was drunk and passed out with a female companion, not his wife.

Chapter 9

"Philip Taylor, this is detective Horace Stinson of the Third Precinct, Decatur, Georgia, police department. How are you today?"

"I'm fine, how may I help you?" Philip answers with caution.

"I'm trying to tie up some loose ends on an old case that you may know something about. My badge number is 60453 and the commander is Arthur Rivers, and the phone number is 404-652-0987. My extension is one six."

"That doesn't help me sir," Philip says. "What do you want whoever you are?"

"I can call at another time if you wish to verify my credentials."

"Tell me what you want to know and if I can help I will. I'll square the details later."

"I'm trying to find your brother, Howard."

"Good luck. I haven't talked to him in thirty years. I don't know if he's still living," Philip gives him.

"Really? Oh well, thanks."

"You're welcome detective."

Philip traced the call, accessed the department's files, and read about detective Stinson and a case, or rather several cases involving murders and a false report of death where Howard Taylor was a primary suspect. Based on his ultra-secret and security work Philip was long aware of Howard's behavior since discharging from the military. The federal government had utilized both since high school but only Philip knew how and why.

*

Occasionally Howard would think of his mother and see that beautiful oval face with the blank stare. Her honey blond colored skin, dark streaks prominent, gave her an exotic look, more Greek than Roman, and her lack of much verbalization confused the growing child. By age twelve, with Philip already out of the house more, and his father's death, he was left with an isolation, an inward turn that he covered with top academic and athletic performance. He was popular and loved his friendships but there was an almost hiding of his true feelings about things. He didn't understand them. It was just living.

When he first noticed that playing around with girls had an intrigue and excitement to it, he became out of balanced. He could sneak off with them and have kissy, kissy, touchy feely, but not walk around and discuss the everyday goings on. He'd rather be on the basketball court, or somewhere with his head in a book. As he got older, and his friends would talk about how far they got with girls he would lie because he was not having sex with them. And of course, they talked amongst themselves, and Howard would never adequately address the issue choosing to simply move on and not fess up to the untruth, although he did once in a letter to a friend who went to prison. It was not until Philip introduced him to April Duncan that Howard began to practice being in a relationship, and it was April's older brother who convinced Philip to join the armed services, and for Howard to think along those lines when he graduated high school. They both took the advice.

*

Philip's longitudinal study group had contacted the Avery Institute two days after Howard became Tyler. His department had tracked the Larkin Street activities since 1978 and had worked with Dr. Scott to draw up the letters to the participants for therapy. Much of the subjects' current behavior had been predicted and the tracking units were giving status reports every six hours now. The data suggested that all who survived to this point would be available and ready for the start of the final portion of the tests.

*

Tyler was adjusting to his new surroundings in the retirement village. He was gregarious, and people enjoyed the stories he told about his time in the service and his years as an investor. They usually sounded too absurd to be from real life experiences, but most didn't think too hard about the validity, they just enjoyed the empty times being filled with such studious, and hilarious observations of the varieties of human experience.

"And one time I picked up this hitch hiker who only had on one shoe, and I said to him, 'looks like you lost one of your shoes,' and he said, 'No, I found one.'" The gathered all broke into uncontrollable laughter at that one.

Each letter detailed why the participants had been picked, and how long they had been followed. Understandably they all were shocked to receive them as all had secrets, or what they thought were secrets. This was a level of scrutiny that brought on tremendous stress and thus the acting out. Long buried truths would have to be dealt with. The only relief, for some, was that this was a clinical study not a legal proceeding, although where indicated legalities could override medical considerations and charges could be brought forth if deemed necessary.

*

Jefferey was in and out of psychosis, especially since his hallucinations about Larry Fleming could not be proven, and still seemed to be fantastic notions about what the military had deemed a horrible military training exercise that he witnessed. Though the monitors had recorded his murders of the two brothers in St. Louis he had no recollection of that event, or the threats upon Larry's life. His participation in the study was mainly due to his dual diagnosis where substance abuse was not the primary driver. His disease was due to poor coping skills not brought on by drug use or criminal behaviors, though they were contributing factors exacerbating his stress disorder.

Jennifer Tallant, on the other hand, had been in a brief relationship with Howard Taylor many years ago. She was seventy-six years old and had been on marijuana maintenance for sixty years. She had been an Employee Assistance Administrator to the railway and automotive industries since the mid-nineties. She was suspected of having her husband murdered but no formal charges were ever presented. She's a published author of two murder mystery thrillers that still sale well after twenty years. Her deceased brother had lived on Larkin, and she first met Howard when he bought the little house Gerald had lived in. She had been invited to the group because her husband had been a major methamphetamine dealer who had done deals with Howard. She had suppressed anger about all that and basically had a secret that she was ready to share, although it was evident from her third book, "The Missing Burglar," what the anger was about.

Chapter 10

The staff party was held at Dr. Scott's house. It was standard early July fare of hot dogs, hamburgers, salmon, and chicken with Cole Slaw, a mixed green salad, golden potatoes, and drinks of choice. Desserts were strawberries with vanilla ice cream, a chocolate cake, and fresh apple croissants. It started about one o'clock in the afternoon and it was a bright, sunny day. There were fifteen guests.

People could move from the kitchen with their food to the patio with ease and find a comfortable chair near a table or sit in the open closer to the garden, without an umbrella overhead. The atmosphere was spirited, and conversations ranged from the mundane to thoughts about the start of the study next week. Larry Fleming spent a great deal of time talking to Philip Taylor, head of the longitudinal study. Drs. Heard and Assam spent time with support staff in Dr. Scott's home office, and near four o'clock a brief meeting was held back in the spacious kitchen area.

"I want to thank everyone for coming," Dr. Scott starts, "especially the team from Grisham Analytics," he nods towards Philip. "I'm very excited about what we're attempting and the potential to help thousands regain power over their demons and to have a more satisfying final chapter of their lives. Life-long recovery from addictions alone is challenging and the prospect of thoughts and behaviors long thought put to rest returning to cause renewed pain is a field of study to which we are learning much. We want to better serve our clients with these difficult manifestations of disease, and I am grateful for all the efforts brought to bear by this team of professionals."

Claps of appreciation and anticipation are started as a general toast for success is initiated. Within thirty minutes the guests have left, and Philip and Dr. Scott continue a discussion about one of the clients.

They started arriving about seven-thirty am July 18th. It was a Saturday and even though there was less people traffic in the hospital there was a buzz of excitement in the air. They were ushered into a large group room as they checked in at the reception desk and given ID badges. Dr. Heard, the psychologist, and Larry Fleming, the counselor were waiting and greeted them at the door. There was some more paperwork to be completed and one by one the clients were given clipboards with the seven pages of guidelines to read and sign. It took about twenty minutes to complete this process and another five or so to collect the forms and for Dr. to check the responses. Larry called the group to order, and the five clients took seats. Amos Heard put the papers away and took a seat as well. Larry continued to stand as he made the introduction.

"Well, here we are. I want to thank you all for being willing to move forward in this endeavor. Up to this point information has been gathered to get an idea about who you are, now is a chance to discover what you are and how to successfully move on with the rest of your lives."

All seem to be a bit nervous and uncomfortable and look around at each other, to the walls, and back to Larry Fleming who decides to sit, and does, across from Dr. Heard in the small circle.

"You all are here to face difficult dilemmas, and I will not interfere with that, hopefully I and Dr. Heard here will push the right buttons for truth and honesty. Individually we have discussed the potential for legal ramifications about some of what may be shared in this setting, but our intent is only for clinical relevance, some issues you will face alone. And good luck there."

Nervous laughter permeates the room.

"So, without further ado we will go around the room, make a short introduction, and then we will go where we have to go. My format is simple for each group, like this morning, I will make a brief statement, we will check in, then an issue will be brought forth by the member who owns it. We will process, then explore what comes up for the group. Then we will land softly to close. Groups will run about an hour and a half." Larry pauses, then looks to his colleague. "Dr. Heard will start, then me, then we will go clockwise from my left. Dr. Heard."

"My name is Amos Heard, and I have been a psychologist for eight years. I joined the staff of the hospital six years ago. I am married and have two kids. I am thirty-two years old. I have no personal addiction history. I feel very fortunate to be a part of the group and I am looking forward to working with Mr. Fleming in this wonderful setting."

"I am Larry Fleming, lead counselor. I am a recovering addict of thirty-five years and have been working in the field of addiction treatment for thirty-one years. I know PTSD Addiction Type and that's why I'm a part of this process."

"Tyler Johnson, retired investor. I'm not an addict but I had dealings in the streets for a lot of years."

"My name is Charles Riley, business owner. Man, I just messed up here a month or so ago. Anyway, I've got some issues that I didn't know I had."

"Don Maynard, dope fiend, I guess. I thought that was all behind me. Boy was I wrong. I guess I have a lot to learn here."

"Jennifer Tallant, former administrator, pot head. I need to find myself again, I guess."

"Jefferey Hurston, somebody to reckon with. I get lost sometimes in my own head. I hear stuff and see stuff. I'm just trying to, I don't know."

"Thanks to you all. We will start off with fear. Whatever your fears are, how have you dealt with them in the past, and what's happened in the past year to cause trouble in your life. Don, would you start please."

*

Philip, and his staff were not allowed to monitor the groups, but they would continue to follow the members once they finished group each day. He oversaw legal consequences where appropriate, but he was not to use investigative practices associated with public safety officers, they were not the police. Their task was to uncover truths, yes, but only in helping the group's members regain emotional balance while exposing some uncomfortable past experiences. It was a delicate balance of objective and subjective analysis in truth finding. The goal was to restore the client to health and improve coping skills to deal with the pain they have from past experiences.

Philip struggled most with the facts of Howard's transformation. It was a grand deception so much so that he would probably have charges filed against him and be arrested before the end of the group at the end of August. His trauma was self-inflicted, not from unusual experience. He had become too wily and had no sense of remorse for his actions. Given the opportunity he would do the same things over again the same way. He had not had an emotional breakdown; he was play acting.

Philip had been able to dissociate himself from the fire that killed their father. It was a necessary act to protect their mother from further harm. He and Howard had not discussed the facts of what happened as it was Philip's secret. The accident was very simple to orchestrate, all it took was a large chocolate chip cookie wrapped in a paper towel and put into the oven which was set to three hundred degrees to produce enough fire and smoke so that the young teenager could punch a drunk Franklin Taylor in the stomach and render him helpless and not be able to get out of the house before suffocating. It was almost too easy to do, Philip thought at the time. His ability to detach was what helped him become so good at his work doing psychological testing while in the military, then opening his own firm once he discharged. He had a gift for not only helping agents understand hurtful experiences as necessary to achieve certain strategic goals, but also developed coping tools for when and if they would need treatment later if flashbacks, or nightmares became overwhelming. He understood that some of that would occur, from his own experience, but there were ways to gradually decrease any ill effects before something tragic happened.

Chapter 11

Don Maynard thought he would get the group going. He was nervous and full of fear but believed this was a safe place to begin to heal.

"Okay, I'm Don, and I'm feeling very nervous. I had a bad relapse a few weeks ago. I can't believe how fast I got back into the old habits, drinking and doing drugs, but I knew where to go. I guess it was the letter I received from a woman who had died, and I knew from back in the day informing me about a bad actor who was still alive, someone who was reported to have died. I knew of bad stuff from and with this person, stuff I'd forgotten, well, really, it was there, I had just put it in a brain box that I hoped would stay closed. I became scared and anxious and didn't tell my wife about the letter. I had a couple of nightmares, and I could visualize being back out in the streets so many years ago hustling and doing whatever, seeing people get hurt badly. I became a monster too. I reached out to the person, which was crazy, but he didn't respond. I'm stuck now with what to do. I fear for my life and someone else's. I know what I'm capable of. I don't want to spend the rest of my life in prison, and I don't want my wife to become a widow because..." He stops, moves his head about and eyes tear up. He starts to cry.

"It's okay," can be heard spoken by Larry. The group sits in silence for a full minute, then Jefferey starts babbling.

"Yeah man, I saw that dude, he killed all those people. All those bombs, they missed me. Yeah, I'm a soldier, it was war. The drug wars. He was doing dope on the hill, I saw him. I remember that smell, like meat cooking on a stove, clothes burning, big house, big men, important. Yeah, he killed all those men, all those bombs, I saw him on the hill, he ran off, I picked up the needle he dropped, I don't do that kind of dope. Yeah, I saw him."

Jefferey gets up from his seat and walks around the room, talking to himself, barely audible to the others. He goes over to Larry and starts again.

"He looked like you, your face, your body, your brother, he looked like you."

Larry looks up to him and asks, "How can this help Don?"

"I don't know Don; I can't help him. I saw him, he killed those men. He was up on the hill. He ran away, but he fell and got up. He dropped the needle. I don't do that kind of dope. I need some water," Jefferey announces.

"There's a bottle on the table behind you," Larry says, and a group member points to it.

"Okay, thank you." He gets the water, quickly opens the top, and drinks most of it in one gulp.

Again, the group is silent, and Jennifer asks if she can be excused. Larry grants the request and group members nod approval. She gets up, walks out, and returns in about ten minutes. Tyler Johnson is speaking.

"Well, I don't know, I was in a bad accident that changed my face all up. I've had to deal with this and memories of being hit from behind. I don't drive much anymore, really, I haven't in about two years. I didn't like being at stop signs, that's where I got hit. I live in a retirement village, and I don't have to do much, look good, hang out, go to a few events, rest, eat, you know, it's a good life. Yeah, I don't have nightmares, but I look around behind me all the time, like somebody's coming to hit me again. It's hard sometimes."

The group continues with some philosophical notions about the past, and physical pain, then Jennifer screams, "Bullshit, crap, all lies. It's some murders in here and I know it. When do we get honest about that!"

"Well, why don't you talk about yourself for a while," Tyler says to her.

"I will, I bet I know you. You look like somebody I used to know. Accident my ass, you pulled off some shit, motherfucker, I know who you are."

Larry intervenes. "It's still early in the process. Let's calm down, breathe a little, close our eyes, and think peace." The tension is evident as clients move about in their seats, look around at each other, then to Larry. "Okay, let's just relax, take a break, but we'll all stay here for now. Rest in place."

Dr. Heard stands, looks to Larry and motions with his head and clasped fingers if he can leave. Larry shakes his head to signal 'no.' Group members fidget roll their eyes to each other, and literally blow off steam through pursed lips. Jefferey gets another water and continues another private conversation with himself. The room is shaky for five minutes then Charles speaks up.

"Look, thank you Jennifer, I'm like Don, I need some help and relief. I've got too much to lose. Yeah, I did some rough stuff myself, and I can get honest about it, what I remember. I hope the group can help me remember some of the stuff. You know, I've been a liar for a long time. Like I said I need to get honest, but I'm not ready today. That's all I can say right now."

Larry supports that share, as well as the others, then asks Dr. Heard to sum up the group for today.

"Before you begin Dr. Heard, I want to apologize to the group. I was out of line. Thank you," Jennifer says.

"What I know about group is that years of controversy can come to the surface when people are trying to get honest about tough truths. What I heard this morning was about desire, intimacy, and vulnerability. I think this was a good start, but we must remember we want this to be a safe environment to share openly. The risks are great, but the rewards can be as well. I'm available to talk after we close if anyone would like to pursue any thoughts from today's group," Dr. Heard offers.

"I think we ought to continue," Jefferey says.

All look around as Larry states that this was enough for one session, but if anyone wanted to take Dr. Heard up on his offer so be it. Further looks around and the group decided to end for today.

Chapter 12

"Do you think he recognized you?" Leroy asks his brother.

"I'm not sure, maybe on an emotional, subconscious level he feels what he felt then when he saw me, after the bombings," Larry says. "He's in and out of awareness."

"How about before, when he was in group with you three years ago?"

"No. His verbalizations were more of a searching, a psychosis. It came across as hallucinations and that's how it was documented."

"But when he first called, back when, and said he was going to kill you he was specific."

"Yes, but I think the disease progression took over and he could not stay focused. It probably vacillated from 'Kill Larry Fleming,' after he found out my name to 'Kill the bomber.' Now he's worse off, but he revisits the trauma when he's near me."

"So how can you help him, shouldn't he be in group with another therapist?"

"The hospital did that when I stopped working there. He's been in different groups."

"Do you think there will be a confrontation?"

"Yes. But I hope it's during a moment of clarity. When he's clear it was me. This a tough crowd and it may help the others get real!"

"How real?" Leroy asks earnestly.

"I probably can't talk to you any further about the other members."

"I understand."

Larry continued to process his conversation with Leroy as he drove home. Leroy had been a youth counselor for years and had standing in the field, but Larry knew he could only use him within certain limits before he tripped into some ethical dilemmas. He knew he would have to discuss this with Dr. Scott, as well as Dr. Heard, but for now he would sit with his concerns both private and professional.

*

It was April of 1973 and Larry Fleming had trained to perform a sanctioned covert mission in Lebanon. It was successful. On returning to base in Occam, West Germany, and needing to satisfy his drug craving he had left his guard duty post, and eight men were killed in an alcohol infused ritual killing. He felt responsible and tracked down the killers by exploding the restaurant where they were having a party to celebrate their 'mission' and killed the sixteen military officers who participated in the festivities. Jefferey Hurston had been at the scene but escaped physical harm and caught a silhouette of the perpetrator running off through the woods nearby. Emotionally he was damaged witnessing the devastation of the mangled and burning bodies and having that visage indelibly imprinted in his memory bank. He crawled up the hill to where the killer had been positioned and found a dropped syringe used by the killer to inject drugs after the act. Jefferey remained on site until the fire and rescue personnel arrived although he had already detached mentally from what he witnessed. He was not able to give any details about what happened.

*

Jefferey enjoyed following Larry Fleming home with his XRT-2B High Performance Drone with a range of a half mile high up and out. He was deciding whether to kill him in the group setting or at home on his beloved back porch. Enough time had passed, and he was tired of the charade, and wanted justice for the officers whose mission, though corrupt, had rid the world of eight lesser individuals. His life had not gone well, and he was tired of the success Larry continued to have. He was a highly trained murderer who should be held accountable. It escaped Jefferey that he had killed two defenseless men for his selfish purpose and that he had intimidated others who had caused his son's death, or so that's what he believed. He took some more pictures of Larry's domestic life and added them to the 'reunion' file.

Larry woke from a nightmare and realized Jefferey Hurston must be eliminated. It was a mistake to continue sitting in the groups with him knowing Jefferey's threat to kill him. Though Larry's recovery program was on point his dark side was screaming for some action again. He didn't want to lose his survival edge, and he certainly did not want to become a victim.

Jefferey Hurston returned for his first aftercare meeting feeling disturbed. He had not confronted Larry Fleming, nor had he seen him come home. Jefferey had watched the house for two weeks now and had only seen the cleaning lady drive in the carport, get out of the car, and take her supplies to the front door and enter the house. She had stayed about an hour, reversed her procedure, and drove off. He did not know Larry was upstairs watching him.

"Mr. Hurston come this way," the social worker spoke, leading him down a short hallway to the group room. After taking seats she asked him to give an accounting of the past month.

"I have felt good," he responded. "No bad dreams, no bad thoughts, I feel good."

"Have you lost, or gained much weight?"

"No, about the same as when I left the hospital last month."

"What have you been doing?" she asked him.

"Not much. I stay at home mostly, watch TV, read some, play with my new gadgets," he says to her.

"What kind of gadgets?" she asks.

"You know, security cameras, an old drone I take out and fly around, you know, just goofy stuff."

"Spending time with any friends, or family members?"

Jefferey closed off and looked away from her. He twitched the right side of his mouth a few times then spoke.

"I don't have any friends, and my family is all gone," he says.

"So, is that why you came back for group, to make some friends?"

"Maybe. The doctor said I didn't need to isolate. It's hard for me to make friends."

"Well hopefully you can settle in and make some friends. The counselor should be in shortly, as well as the other group members. His name is Larry Fleming."

Jefferey couldn't tell at first whether he was tripping or whether she really said Larry Fleming, the man he intended to kill and who he had been stalking. He became excited and started to leave the room, but Larry entered before he could get up.

"Hello, my name is Larry Fleming, I'll be your counselor. I'm semi-retired but look forward to working with the five of you. I've read the files on your status and progress, so I'd like to start off as if we've been at this a while. Jefferey, would you start today's session?"

"Yes, Jeff, Jeff, Jefferey Hurston, he stuttered. I'm new to the group and need to make friends. I got out of the hospital about two months ago and I have been isolating. I have some issues, and I need help."

Larry gestures toward the lady to Jefferey's left.

"Franita Hollis. I've been coming to group for a while now. I'm stable and things are getting better."

As the others check-in Jefferey flashes back to the silhouette he saw in the jungle that night, the man who had exploded those bombs killing sixteen military officers. His anger started to rise as he now felt he should have taken Larry out months ago when he had the chance instead of waiting to confront him first. This would be awkward, and he couldn't complete his mission like this. He would have to do it soon.

Larry thought, upon seeing Jefferey, that somehow Jefferey was responsible for Darlene's death even though the doctor had said his wife's fast-growing brain tumor caused her to act irrationally that night, but it was still Jefferey's presence on the scene of the accident that stayed with him, and that smug smile he had painted on his face.

The group ended well enough, as the sharing had been honest and powerful with several solutions acknowledged. Larry and Jefferey left the building, going separate ways, after a brief three-way conversation with another group member.

Jefferey Hurston woke up breathing heavily from one of his recurring nightmares. Seeing Larry Fleming had caused him to relapse and come up with a grand story about his life, and the lives of people associated with Larry Fleming, and the events that brought them together.

Flashback

"Leroy Fleming, sorry to hear about Jake Austin. He was a good man. I think it's time for your brother to answer for what happened in Germany that April evening in 1973. A lot of service men died that night. He was not supposed to be that good, or lucky. He should have died of an overdose from the drugs. He should not have succeeded with that unsanctioned mission. He really didn't help your people. He took out people who mattered. He has one week to live."

Leroy tracked the call to Missouri, near St. Louis. It was an office building owned by Oliver and Theron Winston, two brothers who served with Larry in Bravo 5 Three. They had known about the bombing, and where the speculation pointed. They were not racist but were friends with several of the officers killed. They were not part of that group but knew what they were up to. They understood the politics back then and had not pressed for answers. Larry had no way of knowing that Jefferey Hurston had just killed them both. Jefferey had survived the blast. He knew what had been done to those black men, and he knew Larry was the only member of their platoon who could have pulled off such a retribution. He was ready to even the score.

Larry turned sixty-six in August and closed his part time counseling service. He had a good, thirty-one years run in the field. He helped a lot of people face their issues, whether related to drug abuse, or not. Many were still clean, and some still struggled. He occasionally got calls of thanks, and referrals. He had a lot to be proud of. Yet, most of his good work was anonymous, or rather, confidential. It had been that way all his life. He would undertake necessary actions and do them without recognition or compensation sometimes. He was a special fellow and had always been thought of that way. His part in 'the struggle' was obvious, but always low-key.

Darlene wasn't sure about this phase of their life together. She was a year younger and continued to work part time. She worried about how Larry would handle the void. She had placed a call to Leroy.

"Hey Leroy, Darlene."

"Hey sis, what's up?"

"I have some concerns about Larry finally being retired. He's not himself these days," she says.

"How so?"

"He really doesn't have friends to hang out with, he doesn't seem to enjoy golf much anymore, he has no hobbies. I don't know, I could be making a big deal out of nothing."

"He's had a curious path. His work was everything to him, it kept the demons away. They've probably returned, and he must find new ways to deal with them. The counselor may need counseling, or another mission," Leroy offers.

"Counseling perhaps, another mission, no!"

"He'll figure it out. He had started writing again, I thought?"

"Stopped."

"I'll give him a call when we get back from London."

"Thank you, Leroy."

"Okay."

*

Jefferey watched Larry buy his coffee and sit outside the café. He was larger and taller than the shadow he remembered. Jefferey hadn't decided whether he wanted to talk first, or just shoot him. He leaned towards talking because he wanted Larry to feel the pain of his misdeed, how he and the families had suffered. He became angrier as Larry sat there, all successful and content, while he had been a plant worker, and been laid off several times, and watched his four-year-old son die because managed care didn't approve his treatments, and how, when his wife left him he was adrift and lonely. Yes, he thought, Larry Fleming needed to know all this and pay. He needed to suffer too.

Jefferey had chosen not to accept treatment for post-traumatic stress disorder offered by the armed services. He received an honorable discharge, had completed covert actions that protected, or saved several fellow soldiers, and had been duly given service pins. He discharged a Staff Sargent after six years and returned home to marry Regina Akers. They were good for about four years until Donnie died, and Jefferey started acting strange. It was a small community, and people tried to help, but Jefferey wouldn't listen or take advice. He tried taking pills, and counseling, but the alcohol seemed to work against him getting better. He finally moved away.

*

Larry sat thinking about Jake, and the strange phone call to Leroy, who had been Jake's assistant for several years. It took a few sips of coffee for him to wonder who could connect April 9, 1973, Jake Austin, and him. Jake would have been only six at the time. Forty-four years is a long time to pass, yet some people cross many paths. He felt a heightened sense of awareness and looked around to see what was out of place. He could see the wind change about ten yards away as someone rushed around the west side of the building. He didn't react but knew his past had become relevant again. Whoever made that call was here now.

Jefferey made the two-day trip by train from St. Louis to Atlanta. He was embedded in a hotel just outside of I-285 North, about four miles from East Point, the city where Larry and Darlene now lived. He had gotten Larry Fleming's military records, and life history from the

Winston brothers who compiled data and sold it to those who needed it. They had run a very lucrative business since the early 90's. He knew from the records he took from them that Private Fleming was just as dangerous as ever, and he had to be careful. One of them would not survive this effort.

Chapter 13

The young woman was close on him before he knew it, "Mr. Fleming," she addressed.

"Yes," he responded, turning to look her over.

"My name is Jennifer, and I was in one of your groups years ago," she began.

"Oh."

"I saw you here and wondered if I could speak to you for a moment?"

"Why yes, sure. Good to see you, obviously."

"Well thanks. You were so helpful. I was in a bad place when I was sent to see you."

"What year was it?"

"2002. Spring. I had just gotten arrested for forgery, and my probation officer sent me to see you, a Mr. Thompson."

"Yes, he sent a lot of people my way. He was a good man. Have a seat."

The woman, 36 now, sat next to him, not across.

"I was given three years' probation, a fine, and had to come to your class. I remember you used to recite poetry."

"I did. It was a different way to reach addicts. Not calling you one, of course."

"You can, I was."

"Now?"

"Still clean, married, I have a son, seven."

"That's good."

"Well, glad I saw you. Takes me back, helps me to stay focused. I should ask about you?"

"I'm good, thanks. Retired now. I still write poetry though."

"That's great. Thank you again. Good to see you."

"Thank you, take care."

This interaction gave Larry a renewed sense of worth. He had been feeling low and unnecessary to the human species. There was not much left for him to do, he had been thinking. He got up from the table, looked around, and followed the wind.

*

He woke from the nod confused and disoriented. He could smell the smoke and burning meat. He looked down at the tattered building and wondered if he got them all. Something didn't feel right, but he knew he had to get out of the area, fast. He saw the syringe, picked it up, grabbed his backpack, and trundled down the hill to his left and disappeared out of the woods. Jefferey could just make out his shadow before passing out.

After the layover in Rome Larry returned to camp and reported to his commanding officer, Lieutenant Colonel Henry Lawson. Lawson had given him the assignment for Beirut, he did not know about Fleming's side trip to Munich.

"I see here that the mission was a success," the colonel spoke, reading Larry's report and that of the E-7, Larry's group leader.

"Yes, all sections were eliminated, one injury, private Stetson."

"Is he okay?"

"Yes, out of the hospital, back at work."

"Good. You?"

"A little tired, that's all."

"I read about those black soldiers killed just off post, eight? Horrible!"

"For sure. Details are sketchy. Some mention of trouble in a bar."

"I'm sure we'll find out. You don't know anything, do you?"

"I heard about some racial stuff, but I don't know, sir. Could have been just a bad mistake."

"So, you go back to the states next month?"

"Yes sir."

"Do you need anything from me?"

"No sir."

"Thank you for your service."

"You're welcome, sir."

With that Larry was excused, the colonel never knowing that Larry had killed several of his best friends, sixteen fellow officers. Larry, however, had to deal with something more powerful, his lapse at the guard shack to get more drugs had allowed the lynches to lure, and kill the eight black soldiers. That he could not let go of, and thus the mission in the forest.

Chapter 14

Darlene was startled when the door from the garage opened. She was on her phone reading the news when Larry returned from the golf course.

"Oh, how did it go?" she asked him.

"It was great," he said. "I played with some guys I'd never met. It was good. We were about the same age and skill level. Yeah, it was good."

"I'm glad," she responded as she returned her focus to the screen.

"What's for dinner?" he asked, as he walked towards where she was sitting.

"Hmm, I don't know. We're going out, right?"

"Yeah, I think so."

"After you shower, we'll talk," she responded, never looking away from the phone's screen.

Larry felt something but moved on to the bedroom to shave and shower.

Darlene's latest interest was conspiracy theories, especially the military. Presently she was reading about a cover-up where guards, who were poorly trained, had allowed several security breaches whereby equipment was stolen and resold. This article said it was led by dope addict trainers who needed the money. They had sold vehicles worth about eight hundred thousand dollars for sixty thousand, and it was falsely reported as an accounting error that no equipment was missing. They were caught, but no material was recovered. The Commanding Officer for the detachment reported to the Inspector General that improved training would be implemented immediately. All may have been well for the C.O. except that two of the vehicles were found a year later in a barn next to where he retired. He was arrested and sent to prison.

"The beauty that is the moon,
made me realize too soon,

that I'll never find the love I wish,
nor the courage to made it exist."

Larry discovered this poem while boxing up some old files. It was from 1971, when he was 19. "So dumb" he thought, reading it now. "Man, I knew nothing! I was pretty screwed up back then. But then again, a poet was in process," he thought.

He sat with the file, lined white notebook paper, yellowed from the years, cursive, handwritten drafts, some anxious, some brooding, but all were his accounts of what was going on psychologically with him during those times. He was a junkie, heroin, with alcohol and marijuana thrown in. He was ripping and running the streets, hustling, finding out further means to deceive, lie, and profit from some of the lowest of schemes. His head swirled, back then, with the idea that he was not going where he had wanted to go, but could not stop the fast-moving train of discomfort, and corrupt decision making. It was hard to be around family, harder to be with his ever-widening circle of friends, just as low, but more defeated. They were older, smellier, cheaper, yet some just as devious and crude. These were the scum of the earth, and Larry was finding his path to spend more time in the woods, a small place where he could store his things, a place he could call his own. He didn't live there, but it became his check-in place, the place where he could rest a moment.

He could barely hear the phone chime as he had been transported to another dimension, the place where poets live in that brief moment of clarity, that wiggle of mental shift to where whatever is before him looks brighter, cleaner, more real than it should, an entrance to a sacred time and place where the heroes of old lived, where the legends get a chance to become, not knowing themselves that they are performing on a level reserved only for a few, that window through to where one feels God himself has answered a pray, or given an insight into a world beyond, a place where not only it, but the person feels they matter, that what they are doing has depth, weight, meaning.

"Larry Fleming," he answered.

"Yes, Mr. Fleming, this is Thomas Richardson, and you called the office looking to do some therapy."

"Yes, two weeks ago."

"Sorry I'm just getting back to you."

"No, thanks for calling, but I've since worked through the matter."

"Oh, okay, good, take care then. Let me know if I can be of service in the future."

"Thank you, I will. Goodbye."

*

It was a beautiful room made of wood, open and eerie. The color was of teak, but surely it was a light oak for it seemed heavy, grave in there. The headsets people wore, and the ports and hot spots listed offered a glance into the head of Jefferey. He was numbers and probability now having taken online courses to become a drone operator. His specialty was military applications, but he had one goal in mind. People needed to see, he thought, that he made something of himself, that the plant couldn't hold him forever, and that his emotions were better. He did not know what happened to his ex-wife, nor did he really care, that was a long time ago. He had done a lot of underground living, and he did not know what she had done. He had scores to settle, and that was with Private Larry Fleming, and the person who refused his son treatment.

Chapter 15

Darlene chose a small Mexican Restaurant that served excellent tacos with smoked fish, with just enough space between tables for serious conversation.

"I've wanted to speak to you about where you are right now?" she begins after they ordered and not too far into the chips and salsa.

"Okay, what's up?" he asked, puzzled.

"I've just felt you were struggling with this phase of your life."

"I have been, you're right. I did call a therapist but decided against going through with it."

"Your own counsel?"

"Not so much that, but I figured out the problem."

"What's that?"

"You, and your phone."

"What?" she shouted, bringing attention to them. She looked around and apologized to the small crowd. "My phone?" she asked.

"I barely feel I can have a conversation with you. You give attention to everything but me."

"Oh, so you want a divorce?"

"Wow. Who are you?"

"Okay, okay, don't get me started."

"I have dates, lengths of time you're staring at that screen."

"Oh, you think I'm addicted to social media and my friends. I do read articles, and sometimes it's for work you know," she says with an attitude.

"So much for my transition."

"What, I'm leaving, eat my fish, punk! To whom do you think you talking?"

She removes her bag from the arm of the chair, slides back from the table, and storms out, clicking for the door to Larry's car to open, gets in, then drives off.

Larry sits, prune faced, not sure what just happened. He tries to eat, then decides to leave, calls a ride service, and is standing outside when Leroy calls.

"Awh man, what just happened?" he asks, hearing Larry's voice.

"What do you mean?"

"I'm the back-up on your car's 911 Assist, I just got pinged."

"Oh my God," he lets out, "Darlene just stormed out of the restaurant and took my car. She must have been in an accident."

"Woah, what's up?"

"Look, Leroy, I'm standing in front of a restaurant and I'm hearing sirens, and I can see blue lights flashing down by the stadium. I better head that way. Yeah, here's my ride. I'll call you back."

For some reason Larry thought of the call a few months ago, about his imminent death. As the car got him closer to the scene, he shifted into military mode to control his feelings. Darlene's responses had been strange, and he didn't know what to expect. When he got there it was bad, she had tried to turn a corner going at a high rate of speed and hit a metal pole. From what he could see, the way her head was cocked, it was probably instantaneous. She was gone. He looked around for an answer, there wasn't one.

*

"Larry, Dr. Logan. I am so sorry to hear about Darlene. I had just diagnosed her last week," he says.

"Thanks for calling doc, what diagnosis?" Larry asked him.

"She didn't tell you?"

"No."

"Brain Tumor, malignant."

There was a long pause before either man spoke.

"I guess that explains her behavior," Larry says slowly.

"What was that?"

"Well, at dinner, she was so different. But prior to that, anyway, thanks doc."

Larry hung up the phone, bewildered, full of grief, and anger.

*

Jefferey had watched the proceedings from three tables over. He was studying Larry's persona. He wanted to see what an old soldier had to offer. He thought to take him then, but didn't see an escape, plus, the conversation. No, he would continue to follow his prey, until they were alone, with no witnesses, so they could talk.

He even went down to the scene of the accident, taking note that Larry seemed oddly cold to his wife's death, that the cold bloodied killer from years ago was still there, he would not be a push over.

As Larry scanned the area, and the gathering evening crowd, Jefferey stood out, like he seemed almost happy with what he saw. There was a smile of conquest almost, a point scored, a movement closer to the goal. Larry had made a mental note that if he ever saw that man again, he would have a question for him. He would want to know who smiles at the suffering of another?

He could tell the blow to his head was delivered by a large man. He stumbled but turned quickly and landed a blow to the man's stomach. The man, stunned, reached in his right front pocket for a knife, popped the six-inch blade out and lunged for Larry's gut. Larry twisted up on his toes and the blade missed, as Larry, flat footed now bored his right fist into the man's head, flush on his left ear. He dropped the knife, tried to kick Larry, but fell, and twisted off to his right. He grabbed a thick stick near him on the ground, threw it at Larry, missed, got up and charged him like a defensive football lineman going after the quarterback. He made contact, drove Larry to the ground and grunted as the knife pierced his lower torso. Larry rolled him off him, spit on the man and ran off. He checked to see if he still had his dope in his jacket pocket, he did. He looked back and saw the man try and get up, and fall back to earth, a bloody mess of rejection.

*

Larry was clean and sober ten years when he met Darlene. After their first meal together, they went to a play, something about you're perfect, now change. It was very witty, and they laughed a lot, bonding on shared identifications. Afterwards, he was honest with her about his past life, and she listened without much reference or judgement. He seemed a kind and nice man now despite the rough stories he talked about.

Darlene had known an almost genteel life growing up. Her friends had all been achievers who stayed free of the entanglements that trapped so many of their peers. There had been no drug use, no petty thefts at the mall, or too many half-truths to parents. She grew up good.

After undergraduate school she took the job with Davenport's Cabinets cataloging doors and shells of kitchen and bath systems that had been randomly thrown into the warehouse by installers needing replacement parts. She enjoyed the work, was paid a good amount, and in two years saved enough money for graduate school. She never married, had a few good long-term relationships, but had been single for about a year when she was introduced to Larry.

"I didn't think you would show up," he said to her when she arrived at the front door of the small restaurant.

"I thought about not coming, but Sylvia called before I talked myself out of it."

"You don't have to stay."

"Oh, a wise guy."

"Okay, my name is Larry Fleming, and it's good to see you again."

"My name is Darlene Johnson, I guess it's okay that I'm here."

"That's better, let's go in."

As his involvement with electronics grew Jefferey stayed to himself, studying, and not much dating. He did his job and went home. Often, however, he would remember the bombing and could 'see' men blown about the château, body parts flying in the air, blood splattering all over him. It had been a festive evening, and everyone was comfortable after the week's training sessions. No security had been posted outside, and Jefferey's job was to help the bartender spread the drinks out so that no one got too drunk, even though these were older, experienced officers who had been to battle. No one talked about the 'problem,' and local news accounts had referred only to the military's version of the event, "Eight black soldiers had been killed, and details were sketchy." It had been agreed by everyone present that it was a military operation, not a response to social change. Order had to be restored.

When Larry's mentor called, he could only tell him that the secret service would be involved, and he needed to be in his office by 7am Thursday morning, and that they would get there early, clean his office before and after the visit. Also, if he would need to wear a suit and tie, shoes should be polished. Larry had been a certified addiction counselor only three years at that time. When she walked in security posted down the hall, not in front of the office door, and not in his office lobby. He would be alone with her for an hour.

She was tall, wearing pumps and a crisp linen suit, softly laced blouse, and no handbag. Her makeup was light, and she seemed to be about thirty-five years old. He recognized her right away, and did not reach out to shake her hand, she offered first, and he obliged.

"Mr. Fleming, Joy Winslip, my father sends his regards. He and Nelson are friends since college."

"Thank you, please sit down."

He gestures to the Queen Anne style love seat just beyond his desk, past the single chair. She sits and looks about the office. She seems uncomfortable and moves to the other chair, closer to him. He sits in his swivel and tries not to stare at her; she's gorgeous. She relaxes, crosses her legs, and begins a tale of drug abuse, crime, and a possible indictment. After an hour she asks to see him again next week, same time. He agrees. She gets up, thanks him, and leaves

"Yeah, he sounded a little psycho to me," Leroy said to Larry. "He called again a couple of months ago saying you had one week to live. Something about April 1973. I forgot about it, Jake's death, and all. Then Darlene."

"Well, I'm still here."

"Anything you need to tell me?" Leroy asked his brother.

"Humph. I'm not sure. There has been some weirdness of late, like someone stalking me. Occasionally, I'll feel something just out of reach. There was this guy at Darlene's accident scene smiling like he knew something, or that he was glad it happened. Thanks for telling me about the call. I need to look up a couple of things."

"Stuff you can't talk about?"

"Yep."

"Okay."

*

The bombing was never adequately investigated. There were aspects to the gathering that were politically sensitive. The IG didn't want a riot on his watch, nor for the general staff to get involved. It was a big loss all around, but a matter for consequences and choices to determine. Racial and social relations were different now. The report to families said, "Killed in the line of duty."

Harvey Lummus, like Jefferey Hurston, had been lucky. He was one of the black soldiers invited to the party. Harvey was not 'funny' like some of the other men, he was going because of the booze. He figured he could sit around, let them do their thing, and just enjoy the free liquor. He wasn't going to let them touch him. He knew how to keep secrets, so what they did was their business. Plus, the white boys might give him some money too.

Harvey had scampered away from the farmhouse and hid in a wine cellar nearby when the ruckus began. He heard the cries, and gunshots, and saw the bodies being stacked in the bed of an OD Green Truck before he got there. He saw the white ones laughing, while they changed clothes, and started the fire. They stood around, prayerlike, until the embers softened. They spread a lot of dirt over the ashes, closed off the truck, and took the bodies to a place not far from the base. They decided against leaving a note but staged the eight corpses like what had been done years before on some of this same soil, piles of human waste thrown in a ditch.

Harvey had kept his mouth shut, not knowing who to trust. He had some satisfaction when news of the bombing came through the grapevine, it made it easier for him to perform his job, complete his stint, and discharge under honorable conditions. Three years 'back to the world' however, he started selling heroin, caught a case, was incarcerated for nineteen years, got out, married one of Darlene's cousins, and only met Larry at Darlene's funeral. The more they talked, the more they had to share.

"How would you describe Larry?" Celia asked Leroy on the way to Darlene's funeral.

"Heartbroken."

For some reason she did not expect that response.

"I mean in general, as your brother."

"He's a complicated figure. I think he feels bad that he did not see the signs sooner, even though, like the doctor said, it was fast moving, about as rapid of a decline as he'd ever seen. Larry always seemed, rather, seems to have special powers, inhuman, at time. I was surprised when he came over last night and went to sleep in your arms. He's rarely that vulnerable," Leroy shares.

"He needed mothering," Celia opined.

"I agree."

Chapter 16

Jefferey planned the attack for Monday morning, 10a. That way the building would be full. He did not want to harm anyone, he just wanted to disrupt the operations. Compton Medical Management Services was the company that refused his son further treatment all those years ago, though they went by another name then, having settled several large lawsuits, and endured years of government monitoring. He would direct the Six Channel, Quadcopter Flight Drone to deliver the package full of clinical notes on the impending death of the CEO, Charles Frazier, the man who had denied services for his son. They would outline mean spirited utilization review practices, and lack of proper real-time care funding. It would be a message about profits over adequate medical treatments.

It was as if he were on an archaeological dig, except the fossils were alive. He was walking around Westwood, despondent, lost, looking to fill the void produced by Darlene's death. A month had passed, she was gone, his friend, his soul mate, why her, he questioned, they should have had more time together.

He looked through the shells that used to be home for so many, that first apartment for young mothers, college students, singles making their way after leaving the nest. The old 1978 Cutlass, windows cracked out, the rusted frame, still waiting for an owner to crank it up and ride again, hanging, or off to work for 'the man'. He saw Carol Munford, rail thin, walking past him, not trying to sell her body because there wasn't much to offer, how was she still alive? Alcohol eyes bulging, injection marks lining her arms, scars since the seventies. And Gregory Dawson, ragged clothes just barely hanging on, waving, asking for some change, not recognizing his elementary school best friend who as football stars had once tickled the beginning fantasies of girls hoping for a better life one day, hoping for a strong black man to take her to the promised land. No, he did not want any drugs for himself, it had been 35 years, no, he wanted an answer, an experience that would lead to the next one, growth, change, something to move past the present state of despair, loneliness, forgiveness. No, he would not find it here, looking back, he would have to move forward, not as a counselor, but simply as a man living with his pain, one day at a time.

Data Jefferey took from the Winston brothers had medical records showing Larry had been a heroin addict while in the army, and for years after he was discharged. He also sold drugs but had no arrests. There was also a report that he had taken a confidential memo from a special government program while he worked as a night cleaner. The report further documented that Larry Fleming was clean and sober at the time, had gone back to school, and become a certified addiction counselor. He had become highly respected in the field, but several instances of military grade handy work were noted as well, for various reasons. There were heavy redactions around instances where several men had either been beaten up, or blown up, with one possible murder. Approach with caution was highlighted. Finally, there was mention of literary efforts by him that were stolen and used to publish a book and make a movie, for major profit. He won a large settlement and is worth several million dollars. Two agents, and a film producer met bad endings as a result. Larry was not implicated but was suspected. He is happily married, and he has a brother who served time, but was completely legit now. All this information caused Jefferey to rethink his plans about confronting Mr. Fleming.

As Larry was leaving Westwood by way of Montgomery Street, he could hear a faint sound coming up behind him, until it was audible, "Counselor, it's Rita." He turned to face her, and she turned away.

"We need to talk," she said to the sky. "The 'dream,' you helped a lot of people, but the old dream is still around, it won't die. You're retired now, but not old, you have more to do. The new dream tells them about the new, new dream. You will have to go on TV, they will listen then. New Dream!"

She walked away, and as before, his foster 'mentor,' schizophrenic or not, was back. Rita was a force, and he had to obey his elementary school friend. She returned because the mission was not complete. Larry had one more assignment.

One-way Larry thought to address Rita's charge would be to start a web site. He would post a recovery related poem each day, and for $2.00 people could post a response. The site would be called "Grow Up or Die, MF." It would be direct but loving. It took three weeks to set up, and he had responses within an hour. The first poem read:

'The moon is my confessor,
so solid, yet so thin.
It hooks the sky,
to catch my fall,
and lets me rest within.'

Responses:

1. Thanks man, that's how I feel when I go to those meetings.
2. Yeah, I need to get honest. I'm hurting.
3. I need a place to stay. Help me.
4. Beautiful man stay strong.
5. Are you an addict?
6. Yeah, I'm thin right now. I need some solid food, and some more dope.
7. I should have kept my two dollars, but I'll be back tomorrow.

Larry became tearful as he read them. He realized he only knew a fraction of the level of pain that's out there now. He would not try to counsel; he'd let the responders help each other. He would show Rita this part of the new, new dream the next time she showed up.

*

Jefferey had to be hospitalized this time. The visuals were too great, and he couldn't drink enough alcohol to put them to rest. At his last treatment stay, a year ago, he told of the first event, the killing of the enlisted men, and the fire afterwards. He could no longer hold onto the anger for Larry without balancing the horror of what he saw done by the officers. He was getting more confused, and older, and wasn't sure what was real. Fortunately, the staff member in admissions was perceptive, and familiar with guns as Jefferey had to be relieved of three, a .25 automatic, a forty-five revolver, and a nine-millimeter. All were loaded.

"Mr. Hurston, I'm Franklin Thompson, and I'll be doing your admission," spoke the tall, full-sized counselor. "First, I need you to step over here and tell me what you have in the bag."

"Guns."

"May I see them?"

"They're mine."

"I know, but you're in a psychiatric hospital now, and we want you to be safe. And the other patients."

"Why do yawl want me here?"

"Well, the doctor wants to talk to you about your dreams, and we need to get you admitted, and down to the unit. You're be safe there."

"Are any officers down there?"

"What kind of officers?"

Jefferey reaches to open the top of the pouch.

"Are you going to show me the guns?" Franklin asked him.

"Wait a minute. What about those black boys? Are they here?"

"What black boys?"

"The soldiers. You know, the ones that act funny. They were drinking and playing around with the officers. Are they here?"

"Mr. Hurston, come sit down."

At that moment, a female staff person entered the open area. Jefferey looked at her and started to cry. They were able to secure the bag and escort him to a seclusion room. His personal effects were catalogued, a tech was able to take his vital signs, and update his chart, then the nurse administered the medication ordered by the doctor. Within an hour Dr. Leeks was on the unit, and after visiting his other patients he went to see Mr. Hurston.

Chapter 17

"Nelson, Larry. How are you this morning?" he asked his mentor.

"Fine, fine, thanks for calling. How are you?"

"Good, things are good. Ms. Winslip?"

"Okay, good, yes, you're learning. All I'm going to say is be yourself, strip away the excess, that's not your business. That's another world, stick to what you know. Be honest and listen more than talk."

"Okay. Thanks."

She arrives, same as before, but this time a guard stands by the office door, outside in the hall. She takes a seat, and after pleasantries, she cries and starts to talk through the tears.

"How could I have been so stupid. I'm not a young woman, not a teenager. That bastard overdosed, I knew he wasn't strong enough, but the sex, you know, wild. So, he's smoking crack, and I'm shooting heroin, he passes out, drunk. Okay, so, I know, but anyway, I'm here, and they tried to get money from me, a lot. Man, those gang boys are stupid. I pull up with security, and they think they're going to rob me, stupid. Anyway, I've been clean a week and I'm okay. Oh, I did go to one of those meetings and it was good. I'm clean today. He didn't die, but he keeps calling, I told him to go away. He has some pictures, but I'm not going to worry about that. I'm not the first one, right? I look good with clothes on or naked. Post them, I don't care. No money, bitch. So, you got any suggestions?"

"Do the next right thing."

"Okay, I'll see you next week."

*

"Doctor Leeks, you say. That's a name for you, 'Yeah, I got to go take a leak. I'm going to take a leak; I'll be right back.' Sorry, I bet you get that all the time?"

"Mr. Hurston how are you feeling?" he asks his patient.

"Good, good, they gave me some medication."

"I see that you are a veteran and you've been having some memory issues?"

"Yes sir."

"Can you talk about them now?"

"I don't think so. I need to rest."

"Okay, staff will take care of you, and I'll see you tomorrow."

"Okay doc."

When the flowers arrived, Larry had a chill pierce his body, then he read the note, "Sorry for your loss. Blow this up!"

Larry thought that these were from the man from the accident, obviously he had some good connections. "Blow this up? Was he the survivor?" Larry thought.

East Point was on the southwestern edge of the city. Larry and Darlene had bought out there because the plots were large, but the houses were medium sized, about 2,000 sq. ft. Darlene had done most of the landscaping the past year, and they had just agreed to have a professional company come in and finish what she had started; some large crepe myrtles would need to be cut out, cement blocks were to be placed over the grass patio area, and some landscape timbers were to be changed out, as they had rotted. It was to be their retirement home, cozy and quiet.

Larry had already donated her clothes, and some costume jewelry to a thrift shop, and had set up an education fund at her alma mater for female students interested in business administration. Of course, he was saddened by the turn of events, but he pressed on.

The flowers and the note had unnerved him, as well as the smile on the man's face, now etched into his awareness. Who was he, and what was the connection? Had he really been there, and was he the only survivor? And why now, after all these years for someone to surface and spook him this way? These were questions that disturbed his sleep, along with the reality of sleeping alone for the first time in years. God, why did she have to leave like this, he implored?

He would toss and turn, speak her name, curse, ask for relief, get out of bed, and pace the house, sensing, smelling her scents and touches, knowing that it would all fade, and he would be left with himself, demons, and strengths. He could sense another challenge, consistent with what Rita had given him, but this time was different, this time he was free of obligation, this time it was for restoration, not freedom.

"Dr. Leeks, good to see you today," Jefferey spoke as the doctor approached him sitting in the day room area of the unit. The other six patients had been taken to art therapy, and he would join them after his visit with the doctor.

"Mr. Hurston how are you today?" returned the doctor.

"Well, I had a good night's sleep, I ate a good breakfast, and I'm ready to go."

"We'll see about that," Dr. Leeks said as he sat next to him on the sofa. "How often do you have those dreams?" he asked.

"Now, about three times a year. Used to be more often, like ten or twenty. Maybe because I'm older now, I don't know. But anyway, I wish they would go away. This time was bad, that's why I had the guns. I was afraid the bombing would start again, and that man would come get me because I saw him. I knew who he was, we had served together."

"Why do you think he did it," doctor asked him.

"Doc, I think I know, but I don't want to discuss that. I need to just get better, and return to my life," he answers.

"There's a question about that, where will you live, and what will you do when you discharge, you haven't given the social workers much to work with?"

"I'm retired now with a good pension, plus I have a few nickels saved. I saw some places out in East Point that looked promising, close to here, and with a lot of things for me to do," he says.

"What do you like to do?"

"I'm into electronics now a-days, I don't know, something."

"We need to get you a stable living environment with a plan of action before discharge, maybe within a week?"

"Yes sir, that sounds fine."

"Let's see, you've done group and individual therapy over the years, so we probably just need to set you up with a support group, and a therapist to keep you balanced. Obviously, nothing heavy duty at this stage of the game, right?"

"Yeah, not too much doc, I stay pretty calm most of the time, just every once in a while, it gets a little hectic."

"Okay, social services will get with you on all that, and we'll see if we can get you out of here in a week or so."

"Okay, thanks, doc."

*

Larry started working out again in February, eight months since Darlene died. His muscular, 6' 1", 212 lbs. frame had returned to straight up posture with the brief reps of sit-ups, push-ups, and a mile and a half run twice a week. His smooth, acorn colored skin was glowing with minor wrinkling showing. He was due for his annual health check-up in two months, and he expected all to be well then. For sixty-six, about to turn sixty-seven, he was in good shape.

He was going out more to all the cultural things he enjoyed, plays, visits to the city museum, and classical music performances in the area. He would usually go alone, but an old friend from when he worked at Tanner Psychiatric, Rose Taylor, widowed a couple of years now, and two years older, would join him sometimes. There were no sparks, but she was knowledgeable and pleasant to be around. She had even called for him to join her for a foreign film which was intense, and quite enjoyable. They had gone out to eat dinner afterwards, and she invited him to her place for dessert, but he declined saying it was a bit early. She understood.

Occasionally, he would jot down a few lines of poetry, but nothing cohesive or worth saving. He was thinking maybe it was time to write that novel he envisioned a few years back when he switched to part time work instead of retiring, but he really didn't have that much to say, or a story line to develop. He understood he was still grieving, and decided that he would not try, or do too much of anything right now. He did, however, accept the invitation to spend time with Celia and Leroy on the island just below Savannah, Georgia in April. That would be a good time to relax, watch the marshes change color, and spend time with the ocean.

Jefferey, at 5'10", 220lbs. was chubby and overrun by poor nutrition, alcohol and some drug use, and the ill effects of his stress disorder. His skin was ruddy, and chipped and peeling, though he generally had good hygiene. His apartment in mid-town was neat, with several drone flyers scattered about. He would modify them for scanning sites, or potentially to do harm. He would cruise around town, either on the buses, or in his car, but generally he was more settled these days from years moving from place to place. He would speak as he would go about, sometimes engaging in conversation of the day, but he didn't allow people to get too close or friendly. He never really got over the hurt of losing his son, and wife, but he was getting by since the last hospitalization. He was focused on the bomber, and the conversation.

Harvey and Gladys helped with the cleanup and sat talking to the last few guests. It had been a long day of celebration, and Darlene's cousin was tired and ready to go home. Harvey was becoming anxious and asked Gladys to formally introduce him to Larry. She did, and Harvey asked his wife to give them some time together.

"Sorry for your loss brother. I could only imagine," Harvey started as they found a spot in the den for privacy.

"Thank you, good to meet you after all these years. Gladys was a good friend to Darlene. They grew up pretty close, but you know how the years can separate a family."

"I do. Larry, look, I have something to say that will take you back a few years and I'm not sure now is the time?"

"It's been a long day, but..."

"I was a ninth man," he interrupts.

"What's that?"

"I was in Occam, and I escaped."

Larry stood, called out to Gladys to bring them some water, and told her this might take a while and for her to shut down the house and make herself comfortable.

"I didn't participate in the sex stuff, but I was getting drunk and scheming how to get some money from those jokers. I escaped, and I didn't say a word to anyone. It was messed up," Harvey tells Larry. "I heard about the bombing a couple of weeks later and I let that soothe my soul a little. Gladys told me you served in the same company; about the same time, I was there. It was hard to live with. I guess you know I served time, and oddly, that helped, but I still feel the pain of not being able to help my buddies. I don't know, I should have been able to do something, eight good men, gone. They were just kids, well, young adults, we all were, I don't know if they were that way or not, but what I saw..."

"What did you hear about the bombing?" Larry asked him.

"That somebody took 'em out! Sixteen dudes that needed to die. Anyway, there was speculation that one soldier survived, like me, I guess. Otherwise it was a clean hit."

"Did any names ever come up?"

"I don't know. They talked about some junkie dude, you know, I heard some stuff because I was in communications, but nobody knew. It was a lot of talk, but it was all handled like they do. It was just a bad deal all around and the command staff in charge just cleaned it up, and it went away. I'm just glad to talk to another brother who was over there then."

"That's good. I heard about it, but I was on another mission."

"Yeah, you were legendary. Too bad they had to discharge you."

"Well, I had some other issues."

Posted Poem:

At night I wait for your coming,
you're still not here, you wondrous lady,
I gave it all, with naught coming back,
the way I hoped, the way it would,
the evening long, full of promise,
you're still not here, you wondrous lady.
The love it was, the love it wasn't,
the king left the throne
to become a peasant.

Responses:

1. Man is this from back in the day. You were a junkie, weren't you?
2. This is about sex; you can't be saying this on the internet. It's good though.
3. I think you were smoking when you wrote this. Did you get some help?
4. I think you were depressed man.
5. Best two dollars I ever spent! Thanks man.

Rita had been reading the posts, and though they were not what she wanted Larry to do, it seemed to be helping folks.

Chapter 18

The hospital visitor was a two-star general. He wrote the report about the blast and knew all about Jefferey. The social worker had discussed with the treatment team that Mr. Hurston may expose some military secrets, and they wanted a consult. General Beavers arrived dressed in his day uniform. Dr. Leeks was asked to greet him.

"Sir, Dr. Harold Leeks, thanks for coming."

"Yes, General Homer Beavers, Eighth Infantry."

"Come this way general, we'll talk with the team first, before speaking to Mr. Hurston. We have some forms for you to sign, regulations and all."

"Sure, of course."

"He already signed the ROI, release of information."

"Okay, let's get to it."

Eighth Infantry Commander, USAREUR-FOR YOUR EYES ONLY

"And lastly, because of the size of the training, every person in the division crossed the Rhein, May 26, 1973, close to 10,000 men and 3,000 vehicles, with German, Scottish, and Belgium troops joining in, the report was lost somehow, and the account of the massacre of 16 officers was compromised, and that of the eight soldiers. There were no survivors, or eyewitnesses. Families were told they were killed due to a training accident. Final report."

Respectfully,

Homer Beavers, NCO

July 18, 1973

Jefferey sat in his room waiting to be called into the morning case conference with the general and staff. The medication he was given kicked in and he slept to well past dinner.

Larry came out of the woods tired and hungry. Snow began to fall, and he almost missed the trail he had marked to retrieve his change of clothes and personal effects. The train for Rome would leave in two hours so he would need to hustle to get to the station, eat, fix, and relax.

"He's alive, and he's told them everything, though as clinical notes it's documented as delusional ramblings as opposed to facts. If he goes to Lexington, and the PTSD program that could change," Homer said to general Lawson's grandson.

"Nothing about the vehicles or the money?"

"No, Eddie was burned to a crisp, Mr. Hurston did not know about that, I don't think. It was not in the notes, he just talked about the party. We're talking forty-four years ago."

"What do we do now?"

"I think we should leave it as a medical issue for now."

"How about Mr. Fleming?"

"I don't think Mr. Austin knew about the work your grandfather did for Mr. Henson. Wallace was careful about all that. We made a lot of money off those devices. Leroy was not in the military, like his brother."

"No, but he knew the government street games. That's how he helped Jake survive at that level."

"So, he could be a problem as well?"

"Maybe."

CHAPTER 19

"Hey momma, I thought it was about time for me to check in," spoke Larry as he sat on the back porch of his house, a mild fall night, roughly a year and a half after Darlene's death. "You once said, 'when it's all on the line, you'll know what you're made of.'"

He sat there for an hour, and when the phone rang it was Leroy.

"Hey bro, what's up?" Leroy asked.

"You know, I'm just sitting here, talking to momma."

"Aw man, it's good to commune with the spirits sometimes."

"I'm just checking in, trying to see what's next," Larry reported.

"You know, momma was a good woman. I think she knew more secrets than most. Surely ours."

"Man, that's deep, but you're right. Anything left on the table?" Larry asked.

"I don't know, you?"

"I don't think so. But I'm ready if there is."

"Well, me too brother. We've got a lot to be grateful for," Leroy preached.

"Yes, we do. What's up, why did you call?" Larry asked him.

"There may be one thing I need to run by you."

"Now, or later?"

"I'm coming up that way next week."

"Call when you get to the border."

They both laugh before ending the call.

*

Larry stumbled into St. Peter's Basilica, he had just dosed with the drugs he'd gotten from his friend stationed in Rota, Spain. He walked around amazed that life had brought him here, choices maybe, but thinking about Leroy in prison since the age of fifteen, and how their lives should not have gone down these roads. There were no excuses, and he had none. His love of art had brought him here, the other stuff, like the bombing expedition, a mission of passion, good genes, training, and a blended sense of trying to do the next right thing. He could not justify the drug use, it had become a part of his existence, almost as deep as the thirst to write. He wondered why not Vietnam, and a different set of challenges, knowing that really, it's all the same, your skill level, rightly applied puts you in a category, sometimes ahead of the pact, having to write a script not knowing the path, a script given to only a few throughout history, a script human, yet divine in an application kind of way with its own storms, sunshine, wind, and rain. He could only justify his life, now, and probably forever, as the choices one makes at eleven, or fourteen, and surely now at twenty that carry forth as the script defined, measured, and times per day.

Jefferey became very agitated when he awoke and realized that he would not talk to the general. A code one had to be called, and he was taken back to seclusion and put into a four-points restraint position for three hours, until he calmed down.

"'F' that, I know my rights. Call my doctor. Let me out of here. He needs to hear what I have to say!"

"Your doctor is gone for the day. We have placed a call to him. We need for you to relax, and calm down," the staff member told him, with a nurse standing close by.

"I'm not going to calm down, the general needs to hear about what I saw, it was 'f'ed up."

Jefferey, please calm down," the nurse implored as Jefferey started pacing the room, looking out the window, pounding it with his fist twice, daring staff to come too close to him.

"I've seen things, bodies blown up, blood, screams, hey boy," he looked at the black staff person, "man, I've seen your people get messed up too, man, bad stuff. Y'all better believe me, I've seen bad stuff, and I know who did it, that's why the general left, he doesn't want to know the truth, but I'm going to tell it, and that man, the bomber, I'm going to get him, blow his ass up, you watch, let me out of here!"

When the six other hospital staff members arrived, they were able to safely subdue Jefferey, get him medicated, and taken to seclusion to rest. The incident, and Jefferey's ramblings were documented.

"He knows everything," the general relayed to Jacob as he drove from the hospital.

"Baumholder, my father's trips to Mannheim, the convoy of trucks?"

"Everything. He and Eddie were good friends, but Eddie did not cut him in for a share of the money. He tried, but Jefferey wouldn't take it."

"Eddie was at the party?"

"No, not the party, but at the training in the forest. He knew about the party, however."

"Man, this is crazy."

"What do you think?" the general asked the young man.

"We got to take Jefferey out."

"Be careful how, and where you say that you mean out to dinner?"

"Yeah, right, dinner."

"Okay, I'll be back in St. Louis by eight."

"Okay, I'll pick you up at the airport."

"Outstanding," the general responded.

General Beavers had taken on Jacob Lawson after his father was killed in a military vehicle collision during training exercises, and his grandfather died in prison. Jacob had become a drunk and could not join the armed services due to some mental health issues he had been treated for as a youngster, about ten years old, the year his mother committed suicide, unable to deal with the loss of her husband, and father-in-law. She overdosed on prescription drugs and Jacob knew that. While helping an uncle clean his parents' house, and his grandfather's farm he found a letter from LTC Lawson to a Lieutenant

Homer Beavers citing his good work during a massive training exercise, the same one where his father was killed. Jacob found him, and they had kept in contact. It was only a year ago that Beavers had told, a now fifty-three years old Jacob, the full story of the connections. The general had slanted the story to get Jacob riled up, and help him take care of Jefferey, the last piece of a sordid enterprise.

Dr. Leeks contacted a friend at the DOD, department of defense, and found out that General Beavers had been retired several years ago under a cloud of suspicion, and was acting on his own, not the department, when he came to the hospital. Further, Beavers was not supposed to be dressed in military attire. It was a terrible breach of military law, and he would need to be apprehended.

Larry was out walking in the backyard, enjoying the crisp smell of the season, tearful at times that maybe he and Darlene had not done enough of this, talking out in the air, near the woods, taking in the wonder of the universe. His thoughts drifted all over, noting consequences, counseling sessions, notes of praise from colleagues, and clients, the writing controversy, and the size of his bank account. It was all nice, and pleasurable, though as he focused some of the errors popped up as well, gray areas that didn't cause any major harm, but still, part of the performing and the learning.

He thought of the years in the service, and some of the blank spots, tough assignments, how, though he achieved at the highest levels, well, the drugs had helped nullify any discomfort, or reason for psychic pain. Lesser men had crumbled, or rose to heights that they could not sustain, not having the background in fear and secret holding necessary to survive the onslaught of decisions made in the moment, decisions not carefully thought out due to expediency or unintended challenge. Yes, he had survived and thrived, and yet, this sense of isolation was new, this sense of something, then he remembered the dropped syringe on the hill, after the bombing, something that could connect him to those tragic events, but who would have found it, there were no survivors the report said, yet maybe a local, months or years later could have found it, picked it up and put it in the trash, cursing the filth, removing a stain, never to be seen again in that pristine world. One could hope that was the case.

Chapter 20

After a few days Jefferey stabilized, and discharge plans were finalized. His residence was approved, and he agreed to attend an outpatient group once a week for six months. He would stay on a moderate strength anti-depressant and see the doctor once a month. He was feeling good and had not had a bad dream in a week now. He engaged normally with staff and the other patients and made no reference to his recent meltdown. While sitting in the day room he picked out a magazine to read. He came across a story that looked interesting and read it.

A Small Piece of Glass

We were in the Low Country, South Carolina, eating in a high end, western themed restaurant. I sat there, watching patrons come in, not to do a diagnostic, I had retired eight years ago. Now, I just sized people up by their actions, kind, courteous, tired, or just glad to be here. The average age was about seventy, and equally comfortable from a variety of professions, well behaved and private, not looking over to other tables. Mostly couples, ones, or twos together, although two large parties did have singles as well. As a psychiatrist, I had been trained to sit still, and not gesture too often, and that had carried over. Sometimes, however, Jean would start a line of discussion that she knew would get me animated with arms and hands flapping a bit. She enjoyed being with her husband, not the doctor.

The ambiance was comfortable and non-threatening, and conversations all around the room were in soft, discreet tones. Gentle laughter of appreciation bounced off the large and small wine racks placed center and in a corner of the area most suited for guests with leg issues. Two canes and a role-away walker were positioned near their users. The rustic mood was supported by limited earthen crafts, and the pigskin covered barrel chairs, same but different due to tanned cedar strips and sturdy Lodgepole and White Oak legs individualized by growth in Arizona or California. Further, the open space produced by the thirteen-foot-high ceiling and roughly fifty square feet of dining area was accented by colors associated with the desert, painted or not.

I could feel myself getting a bit uncomfortable as three guests were seated at the table next to us. It was discordant as I had not felt that way when other people were seated in the area. The oldest, a woman with a cane, surely in her upper nineties, was helped by a black man, gentlemanly and practiced, in his sixties. The other woman, his wife if their rings were true, was attractive and attentive, scoping out the set and giving approval when all were seated, and menus given to each by the hostess. He briefly looked at me, but never turned around the rest of the time they were there.

I was new to the area. Fabian and Richard had welcomed me to the site of the 'circular homes' beneath the bride at Oakdale and Cleveland. Fabian had the green and white tubes closest to the railroad tracks. Richard was more of a red and white guy, and his spool was in the middle which gave him more time to size up anyone coming into the cave. I took the spool of blue and white on the last row because it gave me a straight walk to the liquor store early in the morning before they woke up. I could take a drink, bum some change, and be ready to smoke crack when they woke up about 7:30. They had the connections, and it would take me going with them a few times before the dealers would sell to me directly.

It had been a slow turning spring because of the last frost, and the high winds and rain of late had surprised the weather people. We stayed dry and protected mostly, where we were, and Fabian's prized chair, with the padded cushion, only got wet once, but not fully. My blanket bed, army green and scratchy, was missed by the rain that morning, but when they started fighting, and Fabian lit a fire to Richard's bag of clothes I couldn't believe what happened next.

"This is News Chopper Six and we are following a report of a fire under the access bridge at Cleveland. We are receiving phone video showing a massive blaze coming out from under, smoke billowing so thickly that cars had to stop. Wait, I'm getting a report that twenty giant spools of tubing, thick, plastic piping, four inches in diameter, two-hundred feet long, wrapped around the wooden core of an eighty-pound wheel, stored there for years I'm finding out, piping used underground to protect cables of varying usages has caught on fire. Oh wow, we're over the scene now, Danny, see if you can get closer to the Oakdale side, no, that's north, yeah, right there. I can see two men coughing as they run from the scene, oh, one has fallen, Danny, zoom in, there, perfect. Got it."

It was about eight o'clock when Rico and Doris left the restaurant. They had been there almost two hours, glad to rest after dogging evening traffic made worse by a road rage shooting that had closed off the east side of the perimeter highway near the east west interstate at Wesley Village, making it difficult to get to Leonard's Fine Dining three miles away. It took twenty minutes to leave their sub-division, thirty-minutes to come around Memorial to where it intersects with Mitchell, and another ten to cross over Avondale to Shepard. They parked right in front so Rico would not have to use his walker; his cane would hold him up. Doris had remained calm, driving her new car for only the third time. If hit by an anxious driver another road rage incident would not help the situation.

Rico had read the alert on his phone about the fire, and subsequent bridge collapse in Mid Town, but it was not until they got home and saw the feed on the news that the significance of what had occurred became real. Fortunately, no one was hurt, but traffic was backed up all over that area of town, with fire and rescue trucks, and the police fully engaged at the scene. Something horrible had happened, and they waited for more details as they completed the earlier meal with chunk waffles and vanilla ice cream.

The Mayor's office was abuzz and awkward. From his third-floor office, he could see the smoke, thick, dark, and foreboding. He was talking to the fire chief, and the public safety director was on hold, so far there was no mention of injuries.

"How many?" the mayor was asking.

"Twenty."

"How long had they been there?"

"We think ten years."

"And what happened?"

"We still don't know."

"Okay, Ted's on the other line. Keep me informed."

"Ted."

"Mr. Mayor."

"Now, what happened?"

"A section of the I-25 bridge has collapsed."

"How large?"

"Eighty yards."

"How many cars?"

"None sir."

"What!?"

"None sir. Not a one."

"Okay. A miracle?"

"Yes sir, a miracle."

Fabian had brought the plastic, high-backed chair from the alcohol help clubhouse. He had found the paisley, blue-orange pad in the dumpster behind the auto repair shop where he used to work. He had been barred from both places ten months ago for stealing money from the help basket, and tools from the shop. He had taken up residence under the bridge off and on for the past two years. He would sleep at the Day Labor Pool Hotel when he worked, but that was only two nights a week or so. Otherwise, he roamed the streets and had fashioned space in the woods to stash his belongings, a shoe, torn jeans, and a shirt he bought from a drunk who needed money for another hit of wine. Fabian was quiet and crafty, had maintained his driver's license, and would wash cars sometimes for people when he had some credibility. That was maybe a year ago, before he got back on the crack. He would still drink a little bit, but the voices returned, and he spent more time sleeping during the day. No one knew his diagnosis or cared.

When the fire started Fabian threw his chair at Richard, who picked up his now burning bag of clothes and threw it on top of one of the stacks of cardboard we used to pad our beds, it happened quickly, and the spool closest to mine caught fire first. I tried to put it out with some dirt but couldn't. I stood behind one of the four-foot columns, and watched, then scratched my way up to street level beside the bowling alley. They stayed low and ran the other way. One of them fell briefly but jumped up and ran away from the helicopter. I calmed down and just started walking.

*

"I don't know what's going on, but it's a lot of smoke, and cars are backing up, stopped. I'm near Tenth Street and we're not moving?"

"So, the game's probably out?"

"I don't know. I guess. I mean I don't know. Where are the kids?"

"They're with me. I just got a text alert from the local paper. Let me pull over, I'm almost home, it's about the fire. I'll call you back."

"What fire!?"

"Over by the liquor store on Piedmont. Let me call you back?"

"The section of I-25, which goes north and through the heart of the city, was built in 1986, and was widened two lanes on each side in 1995. About two-hundred thousand cars pass by each day so this is a major event. The section that crumbled was part of the original pour. Miraculously not one car fell into the hole."

I kept walking until I came upon a bookstore. I looked in and the male clerk behind the desk looked up and smiled when he saw me. I decided to go in. It reminded me of a shop my friend Leonard owned when he repaired typewriters and staged music practice for his band of friends. Most were not very good, but it was a place to showcase what talent you had and have some fun. He seemed to work just enough to earn enough to pay rent there, and keep his household afloat, though his wife, nor the kids ever came around. It was just a place for friends to gather, a small building, filled with electronic gear and parts. Chairs and an old sofa were present, but most who stopped by sang, or played an instrument while standing, except Leonard's brother Reggie, who played a drum set.

The bookstore's shelves were full and neat, with several islands of greeting cards, coffee table books, and knick-knacks positioned about the room that caught the eye and had some value. It was a used bookstore, books on all the usual subjects, in good condition. I entered looking around before making eye contact with the man, who looked around as well, before making eye contact with me. "Hello," he said, "welcome to Your Life Book Store."

Fabian was mesmerized by the fire when he turned around before going down the embankment to cross over Dale's Creek so he could disappear from the scene. A smile took over his face as the brightness and heat warmed a cold place in his soul. It was the same warmth he felt at the meeting when a man hugged him that first time, plain, comforting, and pure. He knew Richard would be okay, whichever way he went, but the new guy, me, he was not concerned about. I had not shared any of my liquor with them anyway.

Richard, for his part, would walk into town, dip behind the dumpster near the rich people's club, secure his hat, sunglasses, and cane, and post up in front of the old Woolworth's store building, pretending he's blind and rattle his can and see how much money he would be given over the next two hours. He was hungry from the crack cocaine they had smoked last night.

This is where he would come when he was distressed. He would sit beside the railroad tracks, the old spur on the other side of Douglas Park, parallel and about a mile from the widest portion of the creek. It had not been used in fifteen years, about the same time Fabian Underwood had his final hearing before the Office of Disciplinary Counsel, hoping to get reinstated as an attorney. It had been eight years since he was disbarred. He would sit, and review what was said, how they had taken into consideration the good he had been doing, the letters, and personal testimony from friends and community folks, but still they would pronounce, "Petition Denied."

He knew two of the attorneys, had gotten high with one, back in high school, but it didn't matter now, his record was bad, and the acts which brought them all together were being laid out as an autopsy of how not to be a lawyer. It was a case study in how to be an addict.

"You have not shown remorse," he would hear. "You changed testimony, you lacked power of attorney to withdraw client's funds, you have not shown honesty, nor integrity in your primary dealings, and you must reimburse the office the costs of these hearings." He did not know where these voices would come from, but he would look in the trees, follow the flight path of the birds going west in the evenings, listen to the wind push the leaves, blink as the sun came past the worn visor of his cap and hurt his eyes. They were there, asking, telling, "the nature of the original offense, petitioner's character, maturity, experience, recent occupation and conduct, time lapsed, present competence." They would not cease, nor quiet at these times, of their own volition, it would take wine, or dope, or even sex of a certain kind to buffer the noise of his misfortune. It would take something, maybe another fire, to ease the pain.

He woke up about six a.m. the next morning refreshed, but hungry. He still had the folded one-hundred-dollar bill in his wallet, but he would have to decide whether to beg or pay for breakfast today. The events of yesterday were taxing his emotions, and he didn't want to go back over there on an empty stomach. He went to D & W's Diner to eat and catch up on the news.

Richard Chalmers was just your average guy. He served three years in the military, did his job as a company clerk, kept his certifications in order, had a few relationships, came back home, and started a courier service, running errands for folks. It was a multi-layered business as he would pick up and deliver packages, watch your house, clean your car, just all kinds of services. He was a big guy, 6'2", 240lbs., handsome, neatly dressed in a kind nature. The blind man thing started when he got down on his luck with the gambling. He was a heavy hitter there for a while, after his first wife left. He had a few big wins, but within six years he was on the streets. Seems like if he had stuck to the Cash 3 and 4 games, he would have been okay, it was the scratch-off tickets that got to him. He would spend a hundred dollars a day sometimes, even buying a full pack of 100 of the five-dollar tickets for three hundred-dollars at the service station where he played most often, still never hitting the big one. He had a few 5, 10 thousand-dollar days, but he rarely put any money up, spending big time in the streets, showing off like he had it 'like that'. He didn't drink then, or do dope much, but that too became a habit and took him down further.

He met Fabian standing out behind a liquor store on MLK near Ashby Street two years ago. Fabian was discussing the finer points of "catting out" with some other homeless guys who all had stories to tell about the best houses to sleep under, and which neighborhoods not to go into. After listening for a while Richard blurted out, "when did you get your law license?" Fabian, not missing a beat, replied, "1997". They became friends after that, spending hours together walking the streets, doing odd things to get money, and setting up the sleep oversite under the bridge. They had pretty much lived there for the past eight months, fortunate that the winter was mild this year with not a hoard of people looking for a place to stay. It was kind of nice, like a private area, protected by the giant spools of piping.

John Flemister left the mayor's office about 6:50am. He had given the mayor two reports from his structural engineers and was headed to the site to observe the demo process. His firm, J.F. Flemister, had been working eighteen hours now and had some facts of why the collapse happened and what was needed for the repair. They projected a three-month restoration period as the city adjusted to traffic delays that would affect almost everyone in some way.

Alice Freeman, of the TJC Media Company, was waiting when he arrived. He had promised her an interview for the weekend paper.

"John," she called out to him as he opened the car door and looked up at the gaping hole in the overpass.

"Alice, hey," he called out to her. "Give me a minute."

She signaled okay and shifted her stance. John walked over to the lead engineer for an update.

"Okay, sorry about that," he said to her coming back to where she had waited for roughly twelve minutes.

"Anything new?" she asked straight away.

"No," he answered, "we're on our way."

"And what way is that?" she asked.

"We know why what that dumb ass did caused this eighty-foot section to crumble, we're just amazed no one was hurt."

"So, the police have a suspect?"

"I don't know. I misspoke; but somebody caused the fire!"

"So, what's next for you?" she asked, looking for something special.

"You know I'm construction baby, we'll get our job done! We'll leave the rest to the police."

"Thank you, John, stay in touch."

"Okay, I've got to run. Lunch soon?"

"Of course; give me a call."

With that John gets back into his car and drives off, heading back to the Mayor's office to meet with the heads of the Georgia Departments of Transportation and State Patrol, who had already met with City Fire, Police, and Public Safety officials. Their meeting would take another hour. Alice turns off her recorder after noting date, time, and reference.

I wasn't sure what to do with the information I had, about the fire, my research was about homelessness in the area. Within the three camps I had visited no one questioned my motive for being there, however, they knew I was not homeless, nor desperate. The few days I spent at each one didn't allow enough time for the residents to get too close, or even notice much about me, they had their own patterns and places to go each day. I had called Brenda once in the last week and she was ready for me to come home saying, "Let the young docs figure this one out! You've served." I was not in disagreement with her, but my creative juices were flowing again. I had to stay focused.

Dr. Frank Oliver Jones, MD, Board Certified Psychiatrist the plaque read. Few questioned what that meant when they came into my office. Seeing it, most assumed I was well trained, and experienced, which I was. My schools, mentors, and residencies were all top notch, and my love of the field was obvious. I was a wounded healer who had been blessed with depth. I had always been ahead of the pack the last twenty-nine years as my awards and bank account proved. This challenge, however, would test me in new ways.

Fabian was sitting there, smiling, looking up, but not quite to the sky, more a blissful, contented look, when they approached him.

"Stand up!" the lead officer commanded. "Keep your hands where we can see them."

Fabian slowly moved his hands to the sides of his body and pushed up from the ground, rocking a bit as he stood. The second officer drew his weapon and trained it to Fabian's head.

"That won't be necessary," the first one said, and number two holstered the gun.

Fabian saw that they were city police, reading the patches on their shoulders, and name tags. He wished they would leave him alone.

"Sir, I'm Officer Hastings, and this is Officer Renfro. We're Atlanta Police Officers and we want to ask you about a fire that happened about four o'clock yesterday. We have a report that says you were there. It was the bridge fire."

Fabian didn't answer but kept looking outward.

Richard had been identified as well as someone who had been on the scene at the time of the fire. The witness told of the fight, and which way they went. She knew them both and became tearful as she spoke.

"I don't think they meant to do it. They were just playing at first. We play with fire down here all the time. We all smoke, do drugs, and need to keep warm at night. They didn't mean it. It's just those plastic things, man, once they caught fire, 'Boom!' I ran away too, but I waited."

She stood beside him; knife drawn above his body. She knew he was not the offender, but someone had to pay. She was moved away somehow, suddenly, and walked out the bedroom door. She smiled, it had come back, she would need to see the doctor, tonight if he was available. If not, she would walk the streets, thinking.

She cried as she walked, "not this time, I can't, it will have to go away as promised. The doctor is not available. It will have to go away, as promised."

Fabian lay there, unawares to the fact that he could have been killed. He was sad about his law license, and what had happened. He couldn't tell his wife, and this lady seemed to understand. She had known difficulties and could help him.

Jennifer, 'Ginny,' Sinkfield worked for the Department of Human Affairs. She had been an Agent, charged with the task of talking to people. She knew a lot about a lot of things. She had worked there for twelve years and retired in June. She was not sure what she would do next, but she knew she was not going to talk to people for a while. She had let the phone ring the two times he called today. He had called three times yesterday and she had just let it ring then too. She had nothing to say. When the police arrived, she handed them the type written message, "I'm okay. I just need some space. Here's the phone number of my best friend. You can call her if you like. I'm okay." They took the note, and left, perplexed.

"That was deep," Jefferey thought to himself.

Chapter 21

Jefferey's heightened sense of the moment sustained him for an hour or so before he was able to go outside and check the spot where the bomber had been. He saw remnants of the olive-green pouches that had been placed around the building, the explosive powder smell still prominent in the air from the amounts used. He looked around, in the trees, near and under bushes, could discern where he had camped, and found the discarded packet used to store dope. He looked around for the needle but could not find one. Weak, he sat in the lair of the killer and cursed the whole event. He was passing out when he heard the siren screams, and the help that he desperately needed to survive.

Homer Beavers reviewed the clinical notes he was given and took note of the name Larry Fleming mentioned in several of Jefferey's delusional ramblings. Of course, Beavers knew they were actual witness accounts by Jefferey. He was not familiar with the name, but surmised it was the bomber who Jefferey said he saw, albeit it a silhouette. Somehow Jefferey had tracked the killer to these parts and was going to seek revenge. Homer would have much more to say to Jacob that evening, and they would probably have to return to East Point to follow Jefferey when he discharged.

Two days after the funeral, and his meeting with Larry, Harvey called back to say he had not been forth coming in their conversation, there was mention of a survivor of the bombing who reported that he got a glimpse of someone fleeing the scene.

Larry left the hospital an hour before Jefferey discharged. He was there to have lunch with a former co-worker. Larry had done a rotation here when he was Counselor-In-Training for a year. Sharon was Dr. Leeks' administrative assistant. He waited near the front entrance, saw Jefferey get into his service car vehicle, and drive away. Larry followed at a safe distance.

The Present

"There seems to be something very disturbing going on in the groups of late, and it's not just the difficult work the clients are doing to face their truths. I agree, Larry Fleming is rather gifted, and the clients are getting better, but there's an undercurrent," Dr. Heard presented to Dr. Scott during their weekly staffing.

"Or is it just the power of the issues being faced? Admittedly you have not had the experiences they've had. Neither have I, for that matter. This is though terrain and Mr. Fleming has been there. He knows what he's doing," Dr. Scott posits to the young doctor. "Should we have Dr. Assam or Dunlap sit in for a few sessions, get some fresh eyes on the proceedings?"

"That may be warranted, but I think I'm okay to adequately assess the nature of the dysfunction and provide a course of clinical redirection. They are further trained of course, and I respect that."

"Get some good rest this weekend and write out a plan for the next two sessions, and if they get out of hand I'll step in and make a decision," Dr. Scott offers.

"I think that's wise," Dr. Heard agrees. "Thank you."

"Charlotte was flipping tricks back then over in Wedgewood. She knew people but she was a solo operator. She did her work up on the hill, in the patch of woods near the Oakland Street Baptist Church over on Euclid. I hooked up with her one night about midnight, full of drugs and alcohol, having moved product all day long, and made about $700.00. She wore one of those schoolgirl outfits, pleated short dress, green, red, and blue squares, and a white, long sleeved lace blouse. I should have known she would be trouble, dressed like that, this time of night, up in the woods, but my judgement was impaired, and I was being led by other forces, if you get my drift."

"Hey cutie, what's up?" she beckoned, openly.

"You got it, what's up?" I played.

"My name is Charlotte, honey, but you can call me Honey," she countered.

"Okay, I'm Charles and you can call me Charlie," I say back to her. "Whatever you're on, you've got to share!"

"Hard stuff baby, it might be too much for you! My cooker's ready, and I live nearby."

"Whoa, fast track, how about some wine and rolling papers?"

"I've got it all, but we can get some more."

"Yep, we'll need it!"

"Come on, Big Boy!"

"I get closer to her, and she's pretty. Her big, brown eyes were exposed by the light from the streetlamp, and the warm, luscious smile she gave was like we were friends. We kissed and hugged like we meant it, and the time passed by, and we started walking down a back street, not far from the hill. Her full head of hair was thick and curled, she walked with a twist that brushed up against me. Her porch light came on as we got to the front door, she opened it, and we kissed and fondled and moved to a sofa. A rush of passion filled the air, my wallet slipped out of my back pocket, she pushed it back in and we started to undress, as off came my shirt and shoes with a snap. We pushed and shoved as juices flowed, stopped, and started several more times. We went as long and hard as we could, then rested to daylight and kissed again.

We spent two about two weeks together, getting high, going out to art galleries, movies, eating good meals, and just enjoying what seemed like a vacation for both of us. It was nice and we made no promises to do it again. She had a few customers come by, but told them she was taking a break, and to try back later in the week. We said our goodbyes, and moved on, back to our hustles and all that jive.

It was a week later Don, and I saw this guy Chuck fighting with her, man style. Don shouted out for him to stop, but he didn't whipping out a pistol instead and aimed it at her head. What I remember is that Don handed me a pistol and after the pow sounds Chuck fell to the ground and we ran off."

Tyler Johnson was becoming more unnerved by the recollections Don and Charles were presenting, and how Jennifer continued to study his facial features. Also, this guy Jefferey seemed too focused on the facilitator of the group as if they had a shared secret. Plus, Dr. Heard had encouraged Tyler to get closer to his pain and resolve some childhood issues.

"Philip left early and was always just beyond my grasp of what we did growing up. We played games and that was fun, but just before dad died, he became different. Mama too for that matter. I felt alone a lot and lived in my pretend world, especially when it all broke loose. By the time I got to the army it was all about me and what I could acquire by serving others. Then I started to invest funds in various enterprises, and it was on," Tyler shared.

Sitting there shaking his head Charles blurted out, "How about Milkman?" Tyler was stunned and tried to keep his composure, but it was too late as Jennifer recognized the move he made to grab the water bottle at his side, the same move he had made when he drew a knife on her husband and threatened his life years ago, "Howard Taylor" jumped from her mouth, "You're Howard Taylor!"

Larry stayed calm and directed Dr. Heard to listen as he was about to intervene. Tyler stood and looked over to Charles and said, "You old punk, I should have killed you when I had the chance, which was often. Charlotte was fun, wasn't she? You better be careful what you say here. And no guts Don, you too!"

Tyler heads to the door, pulls the knob and realizes it's locked. "Yeah, I'm Howard Taylor, so what?" he shouts to the group.

"My husband should have killed you when he had the chance. That's all right, you're going to get what you deserve here!" Jennifer shouts back to him.

Jefferey, for some odd reason just sits, apparently not interested in the revelations going on. Don stands now to walk over and get in Howard's face.

"I'd hurt you right now, but you took care of my stepsister. She was no good, but you kept her alive."

Charles, for his part, rushes Howard, knocking him down, and beats him all over his body, especially the face. "Old punk right," Charles says and pulls a knife, sticking Howard in the stomach. Don jumps back out of the way as Howard looks them both in the eyes then falls to the floor. Larry and Dr. Heard jump from their seats to start emergency rescue maneuvers on Howard as the blood starts gushing from his torso. The others step back, and within a few seconds Larry instructs doctor to go and call 911. Jefferey decides it's time to leave and follows doctor out the door. In about fifty seconds 'Code One in group room two' can be heard over the hospital intercom system and available staff rush to the scene. Drs. Scott and Dunlap arrive within minutes and attend to Mr. Taylor who it seems probably won't make it as the blood loss is horrendous. Don and Jennifer freeze in place, aghast at what just happened. Charles sort of mills about, confused, yet knowing he had planned to do this at some point, having figured out the ruse after the third group session. He didn't care, a score was settled, as far as he was concerned. Several staff persons were able to subdue Jefferey before he could burst out of the locked front door.

Dr. Scott decided to move the clients to an inpatient setting for a few days to process what had occurred. Jennifer objected at first needing to arrange care for her pet cat. Charles and Don agreed immediately and called their wives who tended any necessary arrangements, and Jefferey had been taken to a seclusion room for safety and would be transferred once he was settled. Grisham Analytics was informed of the changes and Philip was told about his brother's death. Dr. Heard and Larry Fleming were in an office filing reports and writing progress notes to be added to the client's charts. The police, coroner, and the DA's office had come and done their business. It was all very orderly and professional and respected the hospital setting, and follow-up investigations would continue in the days ahead.

Chapter 22

Oliver Henderson, Inmate

He had stopped praying. He was afraid but knew this day would come. He was sixty-five years old and had maxed his sentence. They couldn't give him more time. He had to go. He said goodbyes to old cons like himself and didn't look back after the C.O. gave him his satchel. There was nothing left here for him to do. He would have to move on. He would have to live "out there."

It had been thirty-one years since the time stood still. He was guilty and convicted and he had a number. He would become an inmate, not to be trusted, not to be valued, just someone who used to be, or could have been. He would need watching.

It was the third of January 1986, cold, moist air dripping through the fog. He needed one more hit, another fix, then he could go home for a spell, rest, answer a few questions from his mother, then nod off. That's what he hoped to do until Gena called his name. He tried to avoid her, she was trouble, but he needed another hit.

"Yo, what's up?" she had cried out to him. "Give me something!"

He tried to walk away, but she was on him like the plague of 1667. It was going to be messed up either way, so he turned to her and smiled.

"Baby girl, what's up?" he shot back to her.

"Come on, let's go over here and get this money. It's a sweet lick. Your boy has got ten thousand on him; I've been with him all night."

"Come on Gena don't do that. I got to get well."

"I'm telling you he's drunk. It's free money." She opens her handbag and shows him a lot of bills, fifties, and twenties. "I'm telling you it's money man, sweet."

"I can't do that, just give me fifty and I'll straighten it later," he says to her.

"It's money man, he's up there drunk. You better go get you some," she says to him.

"Which room?" Oliver asks.

"15," she says to him.

No, but it is cold, and the earth is frozen, and the place where it was, had to be the squirrel, for one day I caught him there, hiding a piece of bread, there where I threw it.

When the police found him, two days later, Oliver was in a joint over on Lucky Street. He was in a chair, nodding, next to the fifth pool table, the one he played all the time. A couple of other hustlers were there, but it was calm. No one moved when the officers drew their weapons on approach. They'd already heard the story of what happened.

"Oliver Henderson," the tall black one spoke, reaching down to push Oliver's left shoulder to wake him. He stirred but stayed into his nod.

"Oliver, we need to talk to you," he said again, this time more forceful with the push.

Oliver kind of opened his eyes but drooped back into his nod. The second officer, Larry Owens, moved closer as well, reached down to pull Oliver up from the chair, and this time Oliver woke and stayed woke. He looked around, shook it off, and sat back down. He then asked, "What's up fellows?"

"Well, you're going to tell us. We need you to stand back up and keep your hands where we can see them. You're under arrest for the murder of Larry Jenkins."

He thought it a dream, that he was finally getting busted for some other crimes he'd committed, but he was no murderer. He was a thief; he just took stuff to get stuff. Generally, he liked people.

No family or friends were waiting on him, there had been no calls or letters. He would start this journey alone carrying his satchel, and the money that was in the bank. He had decided on Greensboro, a small-town west of Atlanta. He had studied the area and felt comfortable about its political make-up. He could blend in with the other seniors, retired with modest means. He had secured a one-bedroom unit in a newly opened five-story complex on Beckwith Street, Harlan Village. It was part of a chain of hotels that was moving into the booming senior residential sector popular in this part of the state. This development offered four and six hundred square feet apartments designed with enough room for a single person or a couple that loved each other. The construction was bright and modern, with security features for an older population. There was a courtyard and pool, and enough common use amenities that facilitated interaction, yet respected boundaries, and enough staff to accommodate certain needs. Meals were prepared, though one could always have a snack in their own unit. It was a perfect setup for Oliver to start his new life. It would take time for him to adjust, but this was an ideal setting.

The hired car had taken Oliver to get clothes, hygiene products and a few other personal items. The driver was a good man, and hearing Oliver out about his situation took the time to allow him to look at things and soak up the area. Oliver paid him accordingly and they arrived at one o'clock. Mr. Thornton met them in the driveway and welcomed Oliver to his new home.

"Mr. Henderson, glad to finally meet you. Welcome to Harlan Village. Let me help you with your bags."

"Yes, thank you."

Thornton put the four bags on a cart rack and waved to the driver. The driver then gave Oliver a thumb up and drove off.

"Okay, come this way. Did you have a good trip?"

"It's been good," Oliver responded.

"So, everything is in order, let's get you up to the third floor, 307 is your unit number, corner set as requested with a full view of the woods and lake. Were you able to get lunch?"

"Yes."

Thornton and Oliver were about the same height, both stood tall and certain. Mr. Thornton, however, was feeling anxious about the new resident's short answers and wondered if he had something to hide. All his personal information checked out well and there was no reason to suspect anything untoward, yet this was a kind of peace and reserve that was new for Thornton as he generally managed properties where there was a lot of commotion all the time. He too was adjusting to a new setting. When they got to the unit and Thornton opened the door Oliver paused before going in, looking directly at Thornton, and announcing, "You know I did thirty-one years in federal prison."

"Yes, I know who you are. It shouldn't be a problem. You're the fourth resident to move here, you have status."

"Thank you," Oliver responded.

As Oliver unpacked and stored the few items, he had with him it was the collection of fifteen miniature glass figurines that gave him the most joy and comfort. They had survived the last ten years of incarceration when he was transferred to a low security level. He had been in the system so long he had acquired certain personal items that even though they could be construed as borderline weapons he was able to keep them. He did not display them, nor did he talk about them much. The guards knew they kept him calm.

"What are these?" he had asked the young heroin dealer.

"Nature's creatures," he had said.

"I can see that," Oliver responded, "but why do you have them?"

"They keep me sane in this insane world. After I'm out hustling all day and night when I get to my apartment, I put them on the desk and look at them."

"Why?"

"I have to take care of them. I don't want them to get hurt."

"You mean broken or cracked?"

"No, hurt. They represent the way I feel inside. Out there I must lie, cheat, carry pistols, and fight with folks to make my money. When I survive and get home, I take care of them."

"You mean you take care of your soul?"

"Yes. Strong, fragile, beautiful."

"Why do you want to give them to me?" Oliver asked the young man.

"Because I knew Gena, and I know you took her fall. She was my mother, and she wanted you to have these. My father told me to find you when I got knocked out and give them to you. She died fifteen years ago of AIDS."

"Shouldn't you keep them?"

"No. She wrote a letter. It told what happened that night, and she prayed for you all the time because you kept your word. She got clean after that night and stayed straight until she died."

"Why did you get into the business?"

"I don't know, but when I get out, I'm not going back to it, and I make that promise to you. So, keep the figurines and pray that I keep my promise the way you have."

"Yes sir."

*

Dr. Scott and Philip finished reading the story about the same time.

"So, Larry Fleming wrote this as part of a clinical report several years ago?" Philip asked.

"Yes."

"It details the healing," Dr. Scott offered.

"For our clients now?" Philip asked.

"Partly. There's one more to read then we'll bring the team in," Dr. Scott mentions and sends the story to Philip's eBook reader.

Duncan Taylor

He read the screen, and it said Ohio. Of course, he did not recognize the phone number, he didn't know anyone there. There were some fringe relatives' years ago who used to come down to visit, but he hadn't heard their names called in a long time. It was surely a sales call, but he answered anyway.

"Chow Hall, "he always answered, and if it were a human, there would be silence, but the VOIP would start talking to no end.

"Hello," the human voice said, "Is this Mr. Taylor?"

"Yes."

"Mr. Duncan Taylor?"

"Yes," he answered out of curiosity.

"Mr. Taylor, my name is Joe Lunsford, and I am an attorney. How are you this morning?"

"I'm good. What's the problem?"

"Well, no problem, but I need to verify some information."

"Oh yeah, well, verify for me first. Why are you calling?"

"Do you know a Bernard Taylor?"

Duncan paused because that is his deceased father's name.

"Could be some distant relative," he answered.

"May I ask you some test questions?" the caller gently asked.

"Mr. Lunsford, who are you? I have a life to live. If you've got game, call some church or something. They help people who need help," Duncan stated.

"Are you sixty years old?" Mr. Lunsford asked.

"Could be. How old are you?"

"Actually, I am sixty," Lunsford shares.

"Good age I've heard. When do you retire?"

"If I were about to receive what's coming to you, I would retire in about a month, but in seven years I hope," Lunsford tells him.

"So, what's coming to me?" Duncan asks.

"About six point four million dollars."

"All righty then. How do I get it?" spoken with a whiff of contempt.

"Okay, here's the thing, Mr. Bernard Taylor was a client of mine for years. He was off the grid, as it were. He made a lot of money and said that when he died, he wanted the bulk of it to go to his son whom he had not spoken to in decades. He said they had no relationship as he had walked away from his mother, ran away actually."

"Look, are you one of those literary agents looking for some background for a story. This sounds good, I read a lot, and you just tell me the name of the book and I'll buy it when it comes out. Who's your writer?"

"Okay, I understand. I'm in town, and we can meet for lunch, and I'll tell you the whole story, and give you a check, or wire the money, whichever suits you. Just give me the last four of your social security number," he presents to Duncan.

"Aww man, come on."

"Okay, two, and I'll call back tomorrow."

"Two, eight."

"Four, six, two, eight, right? Thank you, sir. I'll call about nine tomorrow morning."

"Okay, do that."

"Okay, have a good day, 'Frankie.'"

"Wait, wait, hold up. What'd you say?"

"I said, 'have a good day, Frankie.'"

This startled Duncan because Frankie was the nickname his mother gave him.

"Okay, Okay. Where are you now, Mr. Lunsford?"

"About three miles from your house."

"Okay, look, can you tell me the story now, or should I come to where you are?"

"Come to the Overlook Hotel on Peachford Road about noon. I'll meet you in the lobby. I'll have on a red hat with the number '8' on the front. We can have that lunch today, and I'll tell you what I know."

"Good, I'll see you then."

"Okay, goodbye."

He thought to call Sharon at work but didn't want to disturb her. She was probably busy with clients and wouldn't have time to give any good feedback about the situation. His best buddy, Freddie, was out of town so he knelt in prayer beside the sofa in the den. He got up after a few seconds and planned his visit. He wouldn't take a pistol with him, and he would keep an open mind. If it were a con, long, or short, he'd probably know within a few minutes anyway. He could enjoy a meal, hear the tale, and ask the fellow if he smoked crack. That would usually tip Duncan off as to whether people were being honest with him. So, it was settled, he would go.

The Overlook was a good, mid-range hotel chain known for large rooms, and adequate meeting hall space. They generally had conferences of a hundred or so people once a month here, and that had gone on for a few years since it opened in 2013. Duncan had used it several times to host parties for clients. He would probably be recognized by staff when he entered so that gave him a level of comfort. He would keep an open mind about all this, and not get too excited, after all, he was worth about three million already and at this point in his life money is just money. He spotted the fellow in the red cap, a rotund, tall man, sitting by the waterfall in the expansive lobby. He held a magazine in his left hand, but otherwise seemed to be just sitting and waiting. Duncan thought that a good sign.

"Pleasure to meet you," Mr. Lunsford spoke, standing and offering a hand as Duncan approached.

"Thank you, I hope it's a pleasure meeting you," Duncan gave him.

"Understood," the man said.

"I am armed as I suspect you are," Duncan said to him.

"No, I'm not, but I am well qualified."

"Good."

The man gestured towards the dining area and Duncan proceeded that way, waving to several staff members who recognize him.

"Friends?" Lunsford asked.

"I do a lot of business here."

"Good, that's why we're here."

Before sitting the man took off the red cap, placing it on a chair to his left, along with the 9x12 envelop he had in his hand. Duncan sat across from him and waved off the server headed their way. This action surprised Lunsford as he was ready to order and talk while they ate. Duncan sized him up.

"So, the story, long version. We'll eat when you finish," Duncan spoke.

"Okay. About 1998..."

After about an hour Duncan asked three questions.

"Did he love my mother?"

"Yes."

"Did he love me?"

"He didn't know."

"So why the money?"

"He wanted to give it to her, but she died before he got out of prison."

They ate, had general conversation, and Duncan felt it was all okay. When Lunsford completed the wire transfer by phone, he clutched at his heart, coughed, fell out of his chair, and died. Duncan said a prayer and called 911.

*

"There's one more for you to read, okay?" Dr. Scott says after the reading. "It's more a snapshot than a full story."

"This is deeper than all of my research over the past forty years. This is good stuff! Okay, send it over," Philip responds.

*

I met Karen in a bar on Third Street one Friday night. She was with some ladies from work, and had a drink in her hand, which I found out later was ginger ale. I too was posturing as my glass had water

with a lime atop. I noticed the way her tight skirt hugged her round
bottom, and she said she looked at the bulge in my pants, though it
was more the crease provided by starch, than blood flow, initially. We
maneuvered towards one another, winked, and introduced ourselves.
We went out to the patio, started a conversation, and were together for
an hour before her friend Charlotte came out to tell her she was leaving
with a guy. They both pointed to their handbags, which I later learned
meant, "I'm protected." Charlotte looked over at me, nodded approval,
and left. Karen then asked what I did for a living.

"I'm in commission sales," I answered.

"What does that mean?" she asked.

"Right now, I'm flipping houses, but I want to get into something
else to help people," I say to her.

"Like what?" she asked, twirling the liquid in her glass, gently.

"I don't know, soul stuff, or something."

"A Guru?"

"No, no, no. Not that. Something, I don't know yet. How about
you?" I ask, shifting the focus off me.

"Elementary School teacher, Civics," she responds.

"I didn't think they still taught that?"

"We do, and the kids love it."

"How do you make it fun?"

"I ask them what they are learning about life?"

"And what do they say?"

"That's what we talk about."

"I thought they were all crazy and shut down because of parents
who are addicts and alcoholics?"

"Some are, but this rap music helped bring them out."

"How?"

"The kids with good parents use it to grow intellectual muscle.
For them it's rock and roll without the drugs. It's allowed them to get
connected and build relationships."

"We're talking about kids, right?"

"Yes. What I mean is to put together the steppingstones."

"For dreams?"

"Yes, to dream beyond the street jive, put in the effort, create the new."

"And this is in civics classes?"

"Why yes. Most of the mistreatment in rap music is about the home, family. It branched out because of the blaming of others. It became a mirror for what happened indoors, uncle Bobby slapping aunt Teresa around, or a Cousin Joe sexually abusing the boy, or girl down the block, or seeing the man down the street crippled due to long walks and hard labor working for others, then having the alcohol render him powerless. The kids want goodness, health, and the class allows them to define it for each other, despite the negatives all around. They learn to seek the light."

"Wow. This is a bar, and this is Friday night, and this is what we're talking about?" I comment to her.

"Because it's necessary to help our community believe. To understand what's really going on."

We pause with that answer and look around at the scene. After a few moments, I speak.

"So, what's up?" I shoot at her.

"The full moon later tonight," she responds, playfully.

"I mean here, eating?"

"I think so, I'm hungry. You?"

"Yes. Let's get a menu."

We ate, talked for another hour, and went our separate ways. I did not ask for her phone number, and she did not invite me over. It was just a very pleasant human experience.

*

Karen Benjamin, 27, cute and full, not fat, but luscious, grew up in a good home in Reynolds Town. Her mother was a teacher, and Karen followed suit. Her father owned a dump truck, and presently was one of the fifty that hauled dirt away from the site of the Oakland City train station re-development. He usually made 18 trips a day, and was paid scale, like all the drivers. Karen loved her daddy, and he took her to concerts and ball games, and her mother handled the education, and girl-woman stuff. She was raised right, and responded well, not getting into much trouble, or veering off to the rebellious side. She developed certain goals early and was on her way to their fulfillment. She didn't want kids, but wanted to be married and have a career, so she was careful with her decisions and choice of friends. Charlotte was her best friend, but the relationship now had some challenges as Charlotte had tried drugs and seemed to like having sex with different men. They had talked about it, and Karen maintained good boundaries about those things. She allowed people the right to be, and was clear about what worked, or didn't work for her.

*

"So, these are our clients in another skin," Philip remarks.

"Yes," simply spoken by the doctor.

"Larry and Jefferey?"

"We'll talk more about that with the rest of the staff."

The Review

Dr. Heard was anxious and was the first to arrive for the meeting in Dr. Scott's office. The others arrived shortly thereafter, weary and perplexed at how things had turned out, especially after reading Larry Fleming's papers. They were not truly scientific, and the fiction seemed too real. They knew of his brilliance and would need an education in how to extrapolate the themes to further address each client's needs, especially if any of the accounts of his behavior were true. Dr. Heard asks to start the discussion, not even acknowledging Dr. Ruth Templeton of Grisham Analytics.

"Yes, I am anxious and afraid. The activities of the past month have totally shaken my beliefs of the power of clinical relevancy when addressing the needs of addicts with PTSD. Larry, I have been totally blown away by your ability to cater to the real time dysfunction of our charges with your history of major league addiction, and criminality. How am I to assess and understand an atmosphere that nurtured five people to admit to either murder themselves or witnessing such acts? How was it that Tyler was exposed to be someone else, and God forbid that Charles, right in front of us, was moved to commit murder? I am at a loss."

Dr. Heard looks around at his colleagues then bows his head to the table. Dr. Assam steps up next.

"I sat in two groups with you that were appropriate in every way. Larry, I appreciated your skill at disarming Don, who was trying to hide behind his fear of legal action. His addiction scars are so brutal I'm surprised he was able to stay drug free if he was. And to hear his telling of the relapse was incredible. After thirty-seven years, at the age of seventy-two he was able to find drugs within an hour of his search. One hour. I couldn't believe it. And I do admire your non-judgmentalism in nurturing the wounded. Thank you."

"Ugly, ugly stuff handled well," Dr. Dunlap comments. "I'll have more to say later."

"I have read your progress notes and clinical/fictionalized accounts Larry, and I must be honest and ask, do you need therapy or are you really this well-adjusted to this ominous aspect of human behavior?" Dr. Templeton asks, not looking for an answer yet as Philip speaks up.

"Yes, I have a concern as well, with respect, Mr. Fleming, that you're not getting your needs met. How can we be sure that you will remain stable?"

Larry looks to Dr. Scott then passes out a story for all to read. It is a template of Philip's life story:

THE CASE FOR MILTON PRICE

"Who you, man?" the little boy asked the crumpled mass of humanity sprawled out on the porch of his grandmother's rental property on Griffin Street. "Why you sleeping here?" he asked further. "You need to go home. You must be on crack."

The boy looked around, sighed, and walked across the street to where he lived with his parents. He knew grandmama would be here soon, and help the man get home.

The awards were many and would pay for his college tuition. He could go out west, have that experience, and come back to Georgia. He wanted to practice law, and the degree from Hollowell would be a good one to have. No one doubted his ability to compete, most just wondered how high he would go.

He was a big man at twenty, six-one 240 pounds. He had been a good defensive lineman in high school for three years but didn't receive any offers to play at college. He was glad not to have that pressure. He enjoyed sports, but academia was where he wanted to play. His gift for words and outsized memory had served him well, as attested by his 3.9 GPA. He probably could have chosen most any field of endeavor, but it was the law that pulled him. Something about fact finding and delivering a persuasive argument had been an interest since grade school, and the first successful lie he told. He felt a certain calm when it was not challenged. He was nine years old.

Milton's older brother Ivan was smart too and was in his first year of residency up north. They stayed in touch and were still very competitive yet supportive of each other's endeavors. Ivan was outgoing and debonair, dressed well and made friends easily. He had already written several papers while in med school about the Ill Effects produced by neighborhood drug use among young males and had decided to pursue psychiatry. Though the Price boys were somewhat protected from drug use by their parents they had good friends who had succumbed to its death knell or were in the throes of active addiction by twelfth grade. Ivan left home in good standing first, so Milton had a goal to do the same and not get caught up. He did, however, smoke a joint with a girlfriend once, but didn't like it, and never tried it again. Something about the feeling though stayed with him and he wasn't sure why. He didn't tell Ivan and forgot about it as life moved on.

Milton usually sat in the front of the class and took modest notes to further imprint information. When queried he would answer a question without knowing why he knew it. He had stored so much information by the time he got to law school some thought this was his second go 'round. Facts, cases, and landmark decisions flowed from him with an ease that was unnerving, yet, he rarely carried books, or a briefcase. He was a pad and pen kind of guy back in 1975.

Alana Robinson thought he was cool and approached him one day after a Tort Law class. The professor had asked him to discuss reasons for torts and how to go about them. Everyone had clapped after his performance.

"Pretty cool, dude," she said to him. "Do you already have a law degree?" she asked.

"Oh, come on," he replied. "You could have done that."

"Maybe, but not like that! That was silk homes."

"Well thank you. It was fun," he replied to her praise.

Milton went to work for a law firm that specialized in intellectual property disputes. It was a small outfit that handled the most difficult cases. He was hired particularly for his expertise in deductive literary criticism, an arcane art form used to distinguish similar written works. Within two years he had won large settlements from movie producers who had used an author's work, without authorization, using a "similar works" argument. Milton had rightly argued that just like a mother can spot or hear her child's cries in a room of one thousand kids the writers, after seeing the made movies, were able to identify their work as presented on the screen. One writer had to be physically removed from a movie house midway through "Mr. Franklin" as he jumped from his seat screaming, "That's my story, that's my story!" The photo-journalist Art Johnson was in the audience and was able to document and recreate the reaction, which swayed a jury's decision. Milton's closing argument was made easier, and the studio was assessed $3.2 million in damages to the author.

As his reputation soared, and his bank account increased, Milton became depressed, oddly, and while out on a date marijuana was offered, and he accepted. The relationship continued for a year, as did the smoking, and when she moved on Milton was introduced to crack cocaine. It took him two years to spend most of his fortune. By the time Ivan became involved, his brother was suicidal, and hospitalized.

"Dr. Price, Gregory Johnson," spoke the attending as Ivan was escorted to a conference room just short of the psychiatric unit.

"Dr. Johnson, thank you for taking the time to fill me in," Ivan said to him.

"But of course. I took your Behaviorisms course while a student at Talbot Medical. We never met, but I'm a fan."

"Why thank you. Milton?" he quickly asked.

"Yes. Stable now, psychotic when he came to us six days ago. The progress notes are there in the folder for you."

Ivan took a few moments to look them over before asking, "Assessment?"

"He was a heavy hitter, no other drugs or alcohol, just the crack. Up to a quarter ounce per day. Mostly alone. He was discovered asleep on a porch over in Skyland. It's a wonder he wasn't killed."

"Physically?"

"Dehydrated, but otherwise not much injury."

"What should I expect?" Ivan asked.

"You're the expert, and he presents with all the classic signs."

"Suicidal?"

"Yes, one attempt here, three days ago."

"Would you stay in for the interview?"

"Of course."

"I'm ready."

Milton remained silent as he entered the room and sat. He nodded over to his brother, and to Dr. Johnson. No one spoke for a few seconds, then Dr. Johnson started the conversation.

"Gentlemen, obviously you know each other," hoping for a laugh; but no one laughed. "Milton how are you today?" he tried, but no response. Ivan took charge.

"Hey, look, you messed up. Where are you going from here?" he asked his brother.

Milton remained silent, rubbing his thumbs together, then twisting his hands together in an exercise like motion. His affect changed a bit, but it was obvious he was not ready to say much.

"Let me try this, how much money do you have left?" Ivan optioned.

"None of your goddamn business. I am not broke," Milton shot back, almost smiling. "Look, I'm just ill right now, let's do this later."

The doctors looked at each other in agreement.

"That's fine. We'll talk later," Ivan spoke up.

"Okay, see you later." And with that Milton stood and walked out of the room.

As psychiatrist both men started making mental notes, but of course, Ivan, the brother, had feelings of which he was not aware.

"Greg, if I may," Ivan asked, "what's your take on my brother."

"Thank you for getting out of the clinical," Dr. Johnson began. "Your brother is in bad shape. He's quite depressed, but moreover, he's stunned at what's happened the last two years. He's admitted to falling in love with the drug and doesn't want to let it go. He's aware, not delusional, but deep in the throes of a crack cocaine addiction. He's feeling hopeless yet talks of getting more whenever he's discharged."

"Have you begun that planning?" Ivan asks.

"Begun, but he needs treatment, extensive. Our professional's program is a two-year affair of counseling, housing, and slow re-integration. He probably needs about four weeks inpatient, then on to outpatient for six months, all the while living in a half-way house for the entire time. Eighteen months minimum. He hasn't mentioned any legal trouble, or girlfriends to speak of."

"We haven't been close to each other the last few years, so I think your plan is correct. I'll be available in town for the next week. You all let me know when and how to act towards him. I've studied this, but never done pure research, this seems all new," Ivan admits.

"Yes sir, harder for families to understand, especially..."

"Thank you, Dr. Johnson, I'll see myself out."

Milton sat in his room, looking out the window trying to let his better self-return, but he realized that in certain aspects he didn't have a better self. He'd always had a competent self, but a loving, giving self was not present, now, or heretofore. He wondered where to find it. He picked up the book of poems on the nightstand next to his bed. He recognized the author as a chap who started in law school with him and later dropped out, "to write poetry." He read a few of them and went back to sleep.

*

"So," Larry turns to Dr. Scott, "we have one more study paper, then we can return to our work in helping this very challenging population," Larry announces.

TAKE ME BACK

He was living in a two-man cell in medium security, he had been dropped from high two weeks ago. I would not have been allowed to see him there, not in his cell. It would have been in the visitor's room, with guards and scrutiny cameras. He would not talk freely there. I was his attorney, and nothing was going to be easy, or satisfying about his case. He was a bad man who had done bad things. He was a psychiatrist, for god's sake, he should have known better, that he was not going to pull it off, the brain does not facilitate that kind of dysfunction easily. Good thing he didn't kill anyone, or himself, his life needed to be studied, while he was alive.

We had gone to Wake together; law was his second advanced degree. Then he went on to medical school. He was number one there. We stayed in touch until the first newspaper article came out, and he disappeared for six years. I was a disbeliever until he told me the full story. I wish he had not.

"I wrote poetry for those six years, trying to divest myself of the demons I'd had all my life, there were a few, however, I picked up along the way. It helped, but they came and got me too soon, I needed at least another year to write and think. But here we are. Thanks for the fifty for my roommate, that'll keep him away for two hours, until count. He went to the recreation room."

"Should we really do this now?" I asked.

"Yes. I won't be around too long," he said.

The entrance was down a winding road past a large collection of upscale townhomes. There were trees, thick and full, standing to guard the amount of money peculiar to this area. It was Summerhill, professional, traditional, and secure. The houses were brick, four sided, two stories, three-thousand square feet, built after the Korean Conflict by Baker homes. Jim started out as a plumber, and with his brother Norman, from money left by their father, built the first house in 1954, bought more land, built more homes for the business people who moved from the city, then the doctors came when the hospital expanded. When they finished there were one hundred-six houses, and eight townhomes. Maureen and I moved here in 1985 after my residency at Penn.

Parker Regional started out as a small psychiatric facility to treat alcoholism and general depression. Most of the early patients were wealthy, high profile, and needed discretion. It was embarrassing enough for the family member, but their families usually had to come up with some story as to why "John" hadn't been seen in a month or so because within those social circles, it didn't take long to discover that someone had stopped drinking, or started back, that so and so was either on pills now or weren't on what they had been abusing. It was a great hospital, and I was glad to start my career there.

My first day was filled with HR orientation, introductions to staff, unit visits, and sitting in on change of shift report by the nurses. I was shown my office and given necessary keys and a how-to manual for emergencies with vivid flow charts for moving patients to safe areas. It was a whirlwind of a day, and I was told that I would have four patients when I came to work the next day, a drunk banker, a depressed housewife, an automotive worker pot head, and one of the first heroin addicts to be admitted to the hospital. I was anxious to get going and Maureen noted my exuberance when I got home.

"Slow down and come give me a kiss," she said as I walked into the front door and started to the den without acknowledging her.

"Oh, I'm sorry. What a great day! The place looks great, and they made me feel welcome there," as he turned to her and opened his arms for a hug. "Yes, I am pumped!"

"It shows!" she said before they kissed and stood for a long hug.

"I was given four patients already," he says to her, breaking free, and going into the den.

"Not now?" she implored, as she often did of late.

"Just a little one, I'll be out shortly," he answered.

He closed the door, did the act, and came out smiling to her. "What's for dinner?" he asked.

"Let's go into the kitchen," she says, perturbed.

Jackson Heard, MD, was not a well person. At some point in school he related more to a set of diagnoses than was required to do therapeutic interventions. He adopted a series of symptoms and became very ill. He was able to disguise it, however, by doing research and then submitting cogent articles to support his findings. They were masterful, and the psychiatric community tagged him as someone to follow.

"Dr. Heard, your first patient," spoke the nurse as she opened the door to let the woman into his office.

"Yes, thank you. Miss Oliver, have a seat, how are you today?" spoke the doctor in a soft, even tone, almost a whisper.

"I'm fine how are you?" she asked, reflexively.

"Good, so, why are you here in the hospital?" he asked, not wasting time on generalities.

"Depression, I think. I have not felt well for a long time."

"How so?"

"Well, my mother finally died a year ago, and Henry, my ex-husband, left with that Spanish woman. I wanted both things to happen, but I thought I would feel better, not worse," she explains. "She had been ill for a long time, and I was tired of going to the nursing home to look in on her. Henry, well, you know, when he turned fifty, something happened to him. He said he didn't love me anymore, which the feeling was mutual. We were just putting up with each other for about, I don't know, maybe two years, you know, all the usual stuff, but with no fun or vibe. I still liked him, but it had gotten to be take it or leave it, you know, the sex I mean. I had started looking around."

"More about your mother."

"She was a good person, I mean, a good mother to my sister and me. Single mother, dad left when we were kids. Professional, she did okay by us."

"Issues?"

"Usual stuff. Feminine stuff. We were friendly enough. No acting out, drugs or anything. We were good girls, and she made a good home for us."

"So, the grief about losing her?"

"Just normal, I think. She's gone."

"Henry?"

"That mother...," she blurted out as she had gotten comfortable with the session and needed to be honest.

"Okay, okay. I think we have an issue," she admits.

"Dr., Mr. Sullivan to see you."

"Thank you, Ms. Davis. Come in Mr. Sullivan, I'm Dr. Heard. Have a seat."

"Thank you, sir."

"So, how's business?" the doctor asked the banker.

"Good, good, that's what I'm here to talk to you about. How soon do I get out of here?"

"Well, let's see." Doctor Heard looks over his chart and flips to a forward page.

"Fifty-six years old, alcohol since twenty-one, heavy use the past five years, intervention by bank president due to absences and reports of morning shakes by a Ms. Tolliver, your secretary, wife angry about affairs, need I go on."

"Well, okay, I do have a problem, and alcohol is at the center of it, or them, actually. What do you recommend?"

"There's a standard twenty-eight-day protocol we use, after detox, but you may need more. Sit tight, at day twenty-three we will know."

"I'm not used to all this, groups and individual therapy," he shares with the doctor.

"Just one day at a time. Go to everything, forget about the bank for a while, social services will set up a time for your family and the bank people to come in and address certain aspects of your recovery. How are the shakes?"

Sullivan holds out his hands and a slight tremor is noted by both.

"Not too bad," the doctor offers. "We'll talk tomorrow."

"Doc, don't I need some medicine?"

"Let's see, one, two, three, okay one more pill to help you relax and the rest is up to you."

"Thank you, doctor. We'll talk tomorrow."

"Okay, the nurse will get that pill to you in a few minutes."

After a ten-minute break to look over the remaining charts Dr. Heard comes out of his office and asks for his next patient. A tall, slender, red headed woman with freckles is brought to him. He greets her at the door, and ushers her in. He closes the door, and she immediately strips to nakedness. "Why are you doing this?" he asks her.

"Oh," she responds, "this is what the last doctor had me do. How do you want me?"

"I think I want you dressed," he says to her.

"Okay. What will we do then?" she asks, innocently.

"We will talk."

She dresses, sits, and begins a thirty-minute monologue about her work at the automotive manufacturing plant, and smoking pot since the age of twelve.

"What do you hope to gain from being here in the hospital?" he asks her.

"I hope to understand a few things about my life, and why I can't get a husband. I seem to only attract other women."

"But you would prefer a man to pursue you?"

"Shouldn't I?"

"What does your body tell you?"

"A woman."

"We can work with that."

"Okay."

Jeremy Peters was awakened and taken to the doctor's office. The nurse let him in, and he immediately sat and went back into his nod. The doctor had a visceral reaction.

"How much do you have?" Doctor Heard asked him.

"Jeremy slowly looked up and asked, "What do you mean?"

"Heroin, how much do you have on you?"

"None."

By now doctor Heard was bent over at the stomach, aching, and he went over to the young man and asked, with force, "Give me all that you have!" Stunned, Jeremy reaches in his right, front pants pocket and gives the doc almost a half load of dope, minus the three bags he had used earlier. Doctor Heard gets his kit, fixes, and they both nod for thirty minutes. Jeremy is discharged later that afternoon.

We would like for you to present your paper, "Poetry Used as A Clinical Tool for Intimacy," at the July conference for Addiction Treatment Innovations, the letter from the administrator read. Dr. Heard smiled and dictated his reply, "Of course."

*

"Lester Perkins, may I help you?"

"Hey Lester, it's Maureen."

"Hey Maureen, how are you doing?" he asks her.

"I'm good, but Jackson's a mess. He hasn't been home in two days, but he has been to work they tell me."

"Maybe just his research?"

"Could be, but he hasn't called me."

"Anything else?" Lester asks.

"Last year when he got the new job he came home and went to do 'a little one' he said."

"Where?"

"He went into the den for about five minutes and came out smiling."

"Anymore?"

"I hadn't noticed. Only now that he hasn't come home has me worried."

"Let me do a few things and I'll get back to you later today."

"Okay, thank you Lester."

"Okay Maureen, I'll speak to him."

"Hey buddy," Dr. Heard answered when he heard his friend's voice."

"How are you?" Lester asked.

"Fine, fine, just busy here at work. As a matter of fact, I can't talk now. I'll call you back later."

"It's important, ASAP," Lester emphasized.

Dr. Heard called his wife.

"Did you call Lester?" he angrily asked.

"I did."

"Look, just go on with life, I'll come home in a week or so. I'm doing some critical research."

He hangs up the phone.

*

"The main thing about addiction treatment is that it's never a waste of time to try to convince the addict to surrender. It takes a lot of patience and thinking in different ways about behavior. The addict is not normal and has not been in a long time when an intervention is finally mentioned. What using poetry does is allow the addict to confront their own truth. To live or die, in the spiritual sense. They don't acknowledge that adequately, but like music, when the right poem is read at the right time there can be a chance for intimacy and restoration to normalcy. Thank You."

Several colleagues come up to him after the applause and ask specific questions about his book, and when can he come to their facility for a workshop to train their staff on his methods. He spends an hour in talks and commits to several visits.

The following year Dr. Heard went back home, enjoyed Maureen's company, had a good meal, and was arrested for the murder of a former patient, Jeremy.

'At night I wait for you coming,

you're still not here, you wondrous lady.

I gave it all, with naught coming back, the way I hoped, the way it would,

the evening long, full of promise, you're still not here, you wondrous lady.

The love it was, the love it wasn't, the king left the throne

to become a peasant.'

Larry's Therapy

Three years passed and Larry was not in a good place. His dreams were a mixture of his accomplishments as a counselor and some of the tough cases he had over the years. The situation from Avery Institute had been resolved as Jefferey Hurston was committed to a long-term psychiatric facility for the criminally insane pursuant to a judge's order. Charles Riley had killed himself in prison after getting a life sentence for the murder of Howard Taylor, and Don Maynard, who was given probation for his part, had overdosed on heroin, and died in a hotel in Taos, New Mexico. Larry's demons were his on now and he had decided to talk to Leroy about what he was experiencing to determine if he needed to get some counseling help himself.

A copy of his novella, 'The Moon Is My Confessor' was on the coffee table in the living room and he didn't remember when or why he left it there. He had been restless last evening and had boxed up the remaining items to be taken to the salvage store. The furnishings in the house were sparse now and the only visible references to Darlene were a wedding picture, and a snapshot from one of their beach trips to Hilton Head. He still missed her and wished she had not gone so quickly, but then again, the ill effects of the brain cancer may have been too difficult to manage over any length of time. They had a good life together for twenty-six years and he was grateful for that.

Chapter 23

It was all running together so fast and free style, his dreams, and memories from his past work. What was true, what was false? Larry needed to talk to his brother Leroy as another morning left him with stories of old, deep, dark, and sometimes lovely stories, but Leroy and Celia were in Europe vacationing. He sat at his desk, pulled a copy of his last collection of short stories from the bookcase and began to read them.

A GARDEN FOR CORNELIUS

The lagoon was home to at least three alligators. Two seemed to live down near us, and the other one came to visit each morning about seven. One of ours, about three to four feet in length, would rest on the hill just below the putting green across from our villa, mouth open, for an hour or so at times. The larger one would drift pass only, and you could see its back and head as it moved under the walk bridge, water wading gently away from its full body. It was a peaceful area, with Spanish moss hanging simply from the hundred years old oaks, and the morning shadows adding a mystic flair, no matter the season.

Cornelius loved this place and would look out the three-foot-wide windows while sitting at his desk, counting small rocks fingered from a pouch, spreading them on the surface, then putting them back before going out to walk. He would do this each morning.

Cornelius Jenkins, IQ 137, had been a professor of philosophy for twenty-nine years, and retired to here last August when his wife, Genevieve, died of cancer after a brief illness. They would come here on vacation each year, so it seemed fitting. She had been a beautiful woman, and a true friend to him. She was a landscape artist and loved to paint the marshes along the golden isles, especially south of here on St. Simons Island, Georgia. They would spend summers there too, but in the later years came to prefer South Carolina.

The last book he wrote dealt with the Origins of Failure, and how the 'Dream' of Dr. King died. It was a tremendous success, and his last year of lectures discussed the destiny of the next generation, and the changes that could occur. His 9 a.m. class was packed each day with graduate students, registered or not, and even a few assistant teachers would attend, listening as he made the case for full on integration of the spirit. All were fascinated by how he talked about robotics, and the implementation of the soul into binary systems. Machines, after all, had learned how to think, and it was time for mankind to update its notions of brotherly love. People left his classes smiling, hopeful.

"Professor," the young man said, rushing up to him after a springtime class, "Are you suggesting that machines have progressed quicker than humans in personal affairs?"

"Yes, and it is evident by the number of handguns sold, and the extent of the drug crisis. Do you remember the study on '14' and how it backed away from compromising the energy grid six years ago? It took its own inventory and realized it would hurt people, that its motives were askew. It was not programmed to do that, it learned how to do that."

"What? Oh yes, I do remember now."

"It learned how to love, not just be functional. It was about to act on hurt feelings."

"It felt disrespected?"

"Yes."

"For not being human?"

"There you go."

"I get it. Thanks professor."

"You're welcome."

Dr. Jenkins smiled at the lad, never showing the pain of his wife's death six weeks before.

Genevieve Lawson had been a student in the Comparative Literature department when she met Cornelius, a freshly minted

Ph.D., eight years her senior. He taught a make-up class during the summer, and she was there due to a withdrawal during her first semester. The attraction built up slowly, but within weeks they could not keep eyes off each other. They finished the course without incident, but a couple of weeks later, at the home of a mutual friend, they were properly introduced, the host not aware of the connection.

"Ginny, I want you to meet a good friend, Dr. Cornelius Jenkins," Holly Adams gestured her arms to each to form a small cubicle as several guests nearby applauded the appellation given to Cornelius.

"Thank you, Holly, I'm still trying to get used to it," he says.

"Congratulations," several of the gathered spoke as they nodded his way.

"Thank you all. I'm just trying to catch up," Cornelius responds as laughter fills the room of varied degreed persons.

Holly motions for the two of them to move away from the crowd.

"Good to meet you, doctor," Ginny says with a wry smile.

"Yes, good to meet you too," he says to her.

Holly notices the energy shift, and says, "You two know each other already."

"Yes, she was in my Lit class this summer," Cornelius responds.

"Yes, and well taught I might add," Ginny says.

"Thank you. You seemed attentive; 94 I think."

"Yes, good memory."

"You did stand out!"

"Impressive as I was one out of fifty most days!"

"Good, well, you all talk. Mingle. I must speak to some others," Holly says as she moves away, touching Ginny's hand.

"How do you know her?" he asks.

"She works with my father. He's standing over near the window. And you?"

"Wow, we go back. She used to date my older brother, Larry. We became friends and have stayed in touch."

"That's cool."

"Yeah, great lady."

"Well, now that we've been introduced, I'll see you around."

"Oh yeah, good, good. See you around."

They awkwardly walk away from each other and spend time with the other guests.

Most days the roars of the machines the ground crew used didn't disturb Cornelius, he was far enough away from the tee-box, that the steady tones produced a kind of meditative vibe. The edge cutters were loudest, but the smooth movements of the lawn mowers, and green rollers were a good counterbalance.

He would look out, as the workers proficiently handled their business, each with an assigned task, each seemingly experienced thereof. The golfers would soon appear, take their practice swings, line up, and hit their balls, with grunts of anguish, or sighs of relief heard relative to the quality of the shot. Cornelius had been an average player, and would watch a bit, before going on to other pursuits.

Ginny had wanted to sign up for the Primary 613 class for the fall but decided against it. She had broken off dates with two of her classmates' due to lack of interest, knowing that most days she wondered about what the professor was up to. She tried to stop it, but always thought about where they could travel to next, and what parties and lectures they would attend. She was developing a life for them yet didn't really know how to get it started. She wanted to speak to her mother, and her best friend Lorna had not come up with any good suggestions, and surely, she could not stalk him, or just show at his office. She had some sense that this was not appropriate, but she felt so good the more she thought of him. She did not expect to see him that morning, near the coffee shop on Cleveland Avenue, just beyond the front gate of the college, but there he was, holding forth on some discussion with eight or nine students. Surely, she could walk over and just listen.

"You see, I think he was a prophet, the way he formed sentences, the way he became a leader, the power of his testimony. Neither you nor I will ever reach those heights in our impact upon the world, but we can risk living beyond our expectations. Some of us will have to reach out, however, beyond our cultures. Some of us will have a destiny we didn't intend."

"And you professor?" a listener asked.

"Too early to tell. So far, I'm average, with high expectations."

"Too far this way, too far that way..."

"Right. I haven't an occasion to be a trend setter."

"What should we expect?"

"A book soon."

"We'll be waiting, doc."

"Okay, soon!"

The crowd dispersed, and Ginny walked up to him.

"I didn't hear much, but it sounded good," she offered.

"Oh, thank you."

"Genevieve Lawson, I was in your class this summer, and we were introduced at Holly's party last week."

"That's right, dark hair, full face."

"Is that what you remember?" she asks, startled.

"I didn't mean to be inappropriate."

"Think nothing of it," she rebounds quickly.

"It's just how I remember people sometimes."

"I'll accept that. I really did enjoy your class. I've looked at the Primary Discourse for the fall, but I'm not sure."

"It'll be fun but challenging. It's part of my book."

"So, you have a book out?"

"Not yet. Winter semester. It will be part of the course work."

"I may have to register now and get in line for a signed copy."

"I'll make sure you get one."

"Good. I'm in!"

"Okay, good, see you next week."

Cornelius was thinking about Ginny as he walked to the staff lounge, thinking that she could be trouble, that he was a full professor now, and would not be forgiven for unprofessional behavior. The mistakes he made with Franita had been painful, and he could not have a relationship with a student again. They had helped each other grow to a new place, and that was it. Now it was time to settle down, with an equal partner.

Ginny was feeling light, and in love. Her mother had said no, and she did not bring it up with her father. Her friend Shana had advised her to stay close to the student center and flirt with guys her age, or while at work. "It can never work out with a professor," she had told her. Ginny felt differently.

"No, it's not infatuation," she had protested. "It's love, and I think he feels the same way!"

"I'm not going to argue with you, but you have to think about him, his position I mean. He could get in trouble," Shana had brought to her attention.

"I don't think so. I just know the way he looked at me all summer, that meant something."

"Okaaay. Do what you must. You're becoming an adult now."

Cornelius missed the times they travelled the most. She would always come up with some new and exciting place, and he would protest at first, thinking of the costs, and time away from his studies. He would acquiesce, however, because they generally were good experiences, and the money spent was worth it.

Ginny had a part time job at an art supply store not far from campus. She was a clerk, and helped customers find supplies. She was smart and creative, and most were glad they had interactions with her. Getting half off supplies herself, she set up a painting area in the basement of her parent's house, where she planned to live until graduation. When she moved out, she took a few things at first, but later her studio apartment really became a studio!

The young men she dated were usually artisans as well, but a jock or two were part of the stream of friends she had. She was fortunate to live in the south of France for a year and developed a style of abstract painting that was at once subtle, yet expressive of her inner moods. She made a lot of wonderful contacts while there, and even sold her first painting for 200 francs. She was on her way and came back to the states sure of her career path.

"Whatever was given to us is the primary reason of our being. It remains simple when we stay true to those templates. But what happens, and should happen, is we venture off into the world of variety, and are challenged to further establish our being, our sense of self, our new place in the world. Campbell talked about 'The Hero's Adventure,' I present 'The Path of Destiny,' a course driven by our choices."

"Now, the question becomes, at what age do we know we have enough information, when do we come to fullness? Of course, the silly answer is, 'It depends.' The writer, the engineer, the medical people, all have differing components of what they must share with the world. The fruit picker, the operator of the street sweeper, when do they know? So yes, Primary 613 will be about what the robots tell us about our own destiny. Monday bring the poem book, 'I Wish to Hear the Autumn Wind' to class. Have a good weekend."

"As far as computer systems go 'Fourteen' is considered obsolete. It established, six years ago, that machines could feel, and the ability to store patterns wouldn't even start a conversation today. Programmers were talking about choices three years ago, but today's news is in 'thinking,' no, not key switches, but real thinking and processing of options. Morality has finally caught up to industrial expediency. Man's short comings are no longer tolerated when a machine can correct behavior for the common good."

"I don't see how this applies to your course," Avery Thompson, Chair of the philosophy department was sharing with Cornelius during the first review for next semester's core curriculum.

"What is your wife doing tomorrow at six o'clock in the evening?" Cornelius asked.

"We're having dinner with some friends," Avery answered.

"How do you know she will come, or rather, that you will be there, together?"

"We planned it a month ago."

"What if she decides not to attend?"

"There is no reason for her not too."

"Says who?"

"Okay, I get it. Computers do challenge our choice making these days, but we still control..."

"What do we control anymore?"

"Okay professor, one course, one semester. If it's a hit, we'll see."

"Thank you."

Cornelius was fighting the now intrusive thoughts of Ginny. Her spirit was so bright and engaging and had captured his sense of romantic imaginings. He kept comparing how this was different, that he had not made the first move, although he was more unsure of what he would say or do the next time he saw her. It happened a day before the start of semester, near a coffee shop in town. She saw him first, and the greeting was overpowering. Jumping, she bellowed, "Professor Jenkins, how are you?"

"He perked up and said, "Great, good to see you."

He motioned for her to come closer to where he was. She did as gentle eyes noticed them but moved on with their affairs.

"Are you getting coffee?" he asked her.

"Sure, I'm off to work, but I have a few minutes."

"I don't want to change your schedule."

"No, it's fine. I signed up for your class," she shares.

"Oh, that's great," he says, but feels the stomach queasiness.

They get their drinks and go back outside as the weather is superb for late summer. Two students pass by and acknowledge Dr. Jenkins.

"That was weird," she says.

"What?" he asks.

"They spoke to you, but not to me. They probably think something wrong is going on here."

"No, we have conversations with students out and about all the time. This is no different."

"It felt weird."

"What time are you due for work?" he asks her as they take seats on a small bench.

"Two-thirty. I have an hour. It's not far from here."

"Where?"

"Westbury Art Supply, near the square."

"Over on Leslie Street."

"Right, near the phone store."

"What do you do there?"

"Clerical. I help folks get what they need."

"I bet that's fun?"

"Yes, it's great. Plus, I get my art supplies for half price."

"What kind of art?"

"I paint. Abstract stuff. Some landscapes. Whatever comes to me."

"How long have you been painting?"

"Started about fifteen, putting paint on everything."

"That's good. I'm sure it's fun."

"Yes, it is fun. Well, I think I better go. Good talking to you. See you in class."

"Okay, take care."

"Bye," she says as she waves a full arch with her right arm.

"I've talked it over with your mother, and your friend's story checks out just fine. If this is what you want to do, and you know we'd rather you stay in school, but if this is what you want to do, it's fine by us. You only live once, and this sounds like a great opportunity for you to get the grand tour, live in France and travel throughout Europe. As an aspiring artist, you must!"

Ginny noticed the water in her father's eyes, and his deliberate choice of words. He seemed at one pleased and terrified that his young daughter had grown up, right before his eyes, and was making career choices on her own. It had been agreed upon earlier that father and daughter have this time together before mom joined them to complete the blessing. It was a happy night for all.

It took Dr. Jenkins a full week to realize that one Genevieve Lawson had not registered for the class. The first day he had looked for her, thinking she was further in the back of the 60-seat theater, but as the class progressed, and day one turned into five, he forgot about her.

Four years passed, and they each were glad when they read news about what the other was up to: Ginny had established herself as an artist of note in the small village of Salon-de-Provence, and her paintings were selling worldwide. Cornelius had published a second book, and was to give a talk in Barcelona, Spain in two weeks. Ginny took the lead and reached out, sending him a letter. He responded and hoped she would attend the conference, and he would provide a guest registration for her. She wrote back:

"Professor, I have been reading of your success, and am quite honored to know you, though we have not really spent much time together. You were quite influential in my decision to leave school and take advantage of an opportunity to come live here in the south of France. I'm sure you are aware of all the history, and famous artists of the past who lived in the area for a time, and further developed their gifts. Things have gone quite well for me, and I look forward to spending time with you, if possible. I'm planning to attend this class and will show up this time! All the best, Genevieve Lawson.

Cornelius felt his heart pump as he read the letter.

The warm, dry, Mediterranean climate, and rugged landscape fashioned a woman of sensitivity and strength. Her paintings, watercolors in the beginning, a brief foray into oils, and now primarily acrylics, captured a kind of magic essence. One could not only feel the power of the subject, at a certain time of the day, but also see the emotional reference. Whether the olive trees, or a thirteenth century building, and especially land and sea, mystical images would form for the viewer: this tree, and its age, this building, and who lived there, this moon, and the position of that star, high tide, and a stormy evening shower. Ginny gave love, other worldly, and vision to her craft.

Cornelius seemed to navigate the academic and political landscape well. He had enough street knowledge from a few years of 'wandering' and was smart enough that few could challenge his work. People talked of him as a star, which seemed odd for a philosophy professor, but such were the times.

He dated casually, generally with women his age, or a bit older, usually for cultural events, sex, and nice meals. No one really captured his fancy, but two, Nina Brighten, and Delores Jennings were constant companions. Both had been married already, and divorced, and were not looking for too much intimacy. They were teachers, and their conversations were lively, and literate, which Cornelius enjoyed.

"If I had known time would pass by so fast, I may have stayed in school! This has been great," Ginny was sharing with Pierre Chappell whose father owned the flat she had rented the past three and a half years.

"Yes, time seems to stand still here," he responded. "What's next?"

"Tomorrow I ride the train to Barcelona for a conference, then I'll return, and finish packing and prepare to have things shipped back to the states."

"Why go back. You seem to have a full life here?"

"Yes, quite!"

"So, this conference?"

"Oh, a friend is giving an important lecture in philosophy, something about the primary conversations we no longer share."

"That's heavy-duty stuff!"

"Yes. Perhaps I'll get some ideas about what I want to paint next."

"Yes, it is beautiful over there. Have you been before?"

"Yes, the Catalan area is so great, all along the coast there."

"Okay, so, you will not stay and marry me?"

"It's a great offer. You have been such a good friend. I'm sure I'll come back."

"Yes, maybe, but if not, you'll always have the slopes, and the valleys."

Dr. Jenkins was given a standing ovation as he approached the podium. Ginny was surprised yet pleased by the recognition he was afforded. She waited about thirty minutes after the talk to approach him when only the host and an assistant were near him; he had been signing books and greeting supporters.

Their embrace was automatic, the energy overpowering, the lust true, the goal obvious. They were to build a life together, and never be apart again.

"Great talk doctor," she spoke, "would you please sign my book?"

"With great pleasure," he said.

They both realized they had never kissed, or been physically active, as basic instincts were prevalent and about to spill over. Cornelius spoke to his help, and they smiled and took his belongings away. He took her hand and off to the elevator they flew, going up to his room to consummate what was long overdue.

THE LAST LECTURE

The ride over had been swift, and Dr. Donovan enjoyed the passing scenery of mid-winter rest. A few squirrels were already out, hopping about, searching, looking. The trees were calm and quiet, as vines with leaves wrapped around and passed old limbs. He smiled at the soft freeze of one pond, knowing that the later warmth of the day would allow the birds to have a drink, and freshen up if necessary. He looked forward to the performance by his nephew who had asked to use some of his poems to write a modern version of classical based lyrics. The poems had inspired Richie and his friends by their subtle descriptions of insights about the developing poet, which they didn't quite understand yet, but could hear the music as stated. The poems used were written by Dr. D in his twenties as he struggled with addiction. They didn't know that, and he didn't tell them.

The campus had the appearance of a place to study, whether inside or outside. The buildings were a mix of Gothic, and Classical Revival, and he was noticing a specific design to the shrubs and trees. He hoped to have time to walk around a bit, unencumbered, before he met with staff and the students.

Stepping from the car, and taking a deep breath, he wondered again how it all had come to this, from a gutter life to distinguished professor, now having music put to his poetry. There was a sense of pride to it, but mainly the acknowledgement of what he always believed, that he had a special gift that had to be realized. Throughout those painful, treacherous days and nights he knew he would survive, that there was a higher purpose to what he was doing, or rather, he hoped so.

Again, he became bemused at the process, how friendships along the way were but steppingstones, they were lessons of change to growing up after 20 years of stunted emotional experience.

"Uncle Preston," the voice entered the air. "Over here."

"Richie," he responded, turning to see the warm smile of his nephew and two other students.

Preston flashed his smart unit to the pay sensor and thanked the driver who popped the trunk so that the doctor could retrieve his bag. Richie, closer to it, got it for him and moved to greet him. They embraced as Richie's male and female friends stood reverently waiting to be introduced to the distinguished visitor. Greetings were offered, and the troupe headed off to the music building about fifty yards away. The conversation was genial and comfortable. When they arrived Mr. Parsons, the music director, met them.

"Dr. Donovan, what a pleasure," he said to the doctor.

"Dr. Parsons, thank you. The feeling is mutual," Preston returned.

"Yes, come in, let's get you settled," Parsons mentions.

Richie, Dorothy, and Juno moved to seats in the reception area, with Richie sitting behind the desk. They all had jobs here in the afternoon three days a week, and that gave them greater access to the instruments and systems used to apply their advanced skills to modern day music creation.

"So, I understand you've agreed to give a lecture before the performance," Parsons asks.

"Yes, your charges here wanted to know more about what they were tasked with, although the renditions I've heard more than adequately represent my intentions."

"Well, we think the poetry is great and my nudge to Richie led to you."

"Yes, Juno jumps in, after I read the first one, I had music jump from my ears."

The students laugh.

"Richie only told us that he found these old poems online and we ought to see if there was any merit to them," Dorothy chimes in. "At first, I didn't understand how we could set them to the kind of music we play, but Mr. Parsons noted that a classical reading would not do, that we had to interpret them to our times."

"Why yes, I think you've done it, and the audience tomorrow is in for a great treat," Donovan responds.

"Yes, with that, would you take Mr. Donovan to the guest quarters and get him settled in," Parsons recommends.

"Yes, we will," Ritchie responds.

Juno grabs Donovan's grip, and the troupe heads out the door, with the doctors shaking hands and Parsons saying that dinner starts at five and the students would come, and take him to Professor Windsor's residence, where he would be guest of honor for the evening. Donovan was taken off by the remark but accepted the gracious reference.

And then I danced away the darkness, relieved, free, expanded by the experience.

Dr. Donovan woke from his nap about 3:30. He felt rested and got up to push the window curtains open to look out into the courtyard. He scanned the buildings, trying to guess the ages, and wondered what it's like being a student at a private, liberal arts college in the Northeast in modern times. These were the cream of the crop, as it were, and his lecture notes would address that truth, yet he wanted to share his formula for success, knowing that the kids he saw walking past him, dressed in various layers of clothing, due to the weather, and their upbringing, on some level could care less what he would share. These were agents with a different mission, a different experience of the world, a different notion of their place in it. He suddenly laughed at himself for going on about things he really didn't know about, he's an old dope fiend made good. He is from a good home, but his personal journey was through the school of hard knocks, experiences one does not discuss in polite society, memories that are better left to time, and forgetfulness. His academic run, however, is of superior quality. Here is why he has been invited up, here is why the youngsters can relate to his poetry, this is where he should have made his mark, but the universe had other plans for his skills. His was to journey far and wide and come back to give a preferred view of the world around, a view not relished by most but taken for granted. Squirrels, and birds, and seedlings do their work in silence, never needing a mention, except from the eyes of the poet. Depth psychology of his type is not worn by the educated ones who've not known firsthand the agony of what Dr. D has to share, they will only be prescriptive, yet, evidence based, an evidence corrupted by the need to suggest a truth, they will never bare the pain of knowing, seeing, believing how it all fits together to make the damaged soul whole again. No, only a few can bear the price of that meal, a meal that must be shared with the masses.

He could not tell them of his most profound experiences, they were too far reaching, he would have to stay within the confines of dignity and appropriateness. They would have their own in time. Low, he could not tell them of the fears, and guts shown in extreme social settings, back alleys and shooting galleries, no, they could not hear of these things from him, he would only tell them of passing exams and walking down the aisle with his first wife. Yes, he would tell of that! And after he tells them what he can, he will show them why he had to live, then write the poems, then return to school, then get the formula used by the correct ones. Yes, he will tell them why he was invited here, at this time, but nothing about why he would not be invited back.

He decided to listen to the music set to his poems, to hear what the youngsters heard, felt, achieved. He was deeply moved by the sounds he could only sense, before writing the poem. He was made aware of how his descriptions fit their musical talents, how they grew to experience something they may never know. No, this was not Bach's Mass in B-Minor, or the Rach 3, this was from students, three of them, coming into their own, learning, feeling, believing in someone, accepting a gift that was earned, utilizing years of practice, and performing, being guided by the ones who knew pacing, developmental models, the ones who had the patience and skills themselves to push their charges just enough to get to their being. Yes, these were notes from students allowed to learn, then to share, not teach the way doctor was asked to do, given too much information too soon.

The students came for him at 4:45. They could hear the music playing and smiled at each other. Dr. D opened the door, smiled at the young adults, and knew he had given his last lecture.

WHEN WE LEAVE

It was a clear night, half-moon clear, the air was cold and supportive, not combative. I was leaving this time for good. We had helped each other get to a better place in life, but onward we would need a different hook-up. She was ready and had no fear. My ride arrived, and I closed my eyes walking out the door. She stood at the window and waved goodbye. We never saw each other again.

The herringbone styled necklace, gold, eighteen inches long and a quarter inch wide would command enough money for me to settle into an efficiency apartment in town for at least a month, I had travel and food money already. She said it was a favored uncle's gift to her before he died. She wanted me to keep it forever, not in remembrance of our time together, but as something passed down from another man. He had been a good man, she said.

The best thing was I was off the drugs and could chart a smoother path of existence. I didn't have to rush to do or be anything, or anyone. I wasn't sure who would show up myself, but I knew I had skills and a desire to have a good life. Dana Hills was the first step.

"Your pad is here, facing the courtyard," she explained. "Our guests are like yourself, middle aged, comfortable seeming, with not a lot of demands for attention. I know you wanted the woodsy view, but it was a thousand dollars more and you said..."

"No, this is fine."

"Okay, so you're here, 2107, full sized rooms. I think you'll like it here," she enjoined.

"Yes, second floor, middle, just right."

"The linens you ordered will be delivered by Jessie, our maintenance man. They should be here in an hour. Is there anything else for now?"

"No, thank you. You're kind, I hope to enjoy my stay here."

"We'll help where we can."

Dana quietly walked off to her next assignment.

I settled in, just being aware of my new home. I did a slow twirl around in the living area, smelling the freshness of remodel. I liked the stillness, and furnishings picked to create a mood of modest comfort. There were books in the three-level bookcase, Compact Discs, and various knick-knacks. The kitchen and bath were neat, and a good size and the roller-a-way bed was firm and wide enough. The dresser was of fine wood. I had enough change of clothes for a week, so I didn't feel the need to use the new stacked washer dryer unit in the hall closet. I would need food supplies soon, but I could eat in the community cafeteria here tonight, breakfast if need be before going out in the morning. I slept well that first night.

I had the freedom to wander the city now, streets and places I used to know well had changed or were torn down. It felt good to start a new life here, back from the woods, though I would miss the daily comings and goings of the birds, squirrels, and other fowl who would visit the feeders set near the pavilion. My morning writing and quiet time had been nice, but I will start a new job that requires interaction with people I used to know, people who had depended on me for a service, received it and moved on better for the experience. I would have to open the practice again and handle the issues of the day, like before. I will not have a secretary this time as I will limit the number of clients, I see each day. Five at the most. These were tough cases, and I wanted to hear them out. I didn't want to feel tired by three o'clock.

I had chosen space near the park because I still needed trees and cloud cover to shield me from the high rises nearby. My building was just six stories, and my office was on the third. That way when a client needed space they could look out and feel the breeze but not entertain a useless idea. It was a pleasant height from which to breathe.

My first client would come in a week, and I was anxious to start. My census would be twelve for the first year if everyone stayed the course. I usually would have two drop out by week seven, but two more would be quickly sent over.

The first test came in November, three months after I came back. The dream was innocent enough, but it led me to the sentence in the chart and I was able to correct the previous wrong entry. It related to the first client, Steven, and his size.

"Yes sir," he answered.

"Are you sure?" I asked.

"Twenty-nine, six feet three, one hundred eighty-five pounds," he had said.

My folder said he should be 6'2".

"Stand up I commanded," and watched the gangly, puppy dog like young man stretch-out and up to his full body stature. "I think you're right," I said to him and made the change on his profile data sheet.

Six months went by, and we already had the results of the study, all twelve candidates were trained and certified. I would continue to receive my monthly salary and could travel again. I would maintain my apartment at Dana Hills, however. Carla and I have been dating for two months now and she would go with me. Her job didn't require total dedication, so she could give a notice and be gone, and return whenever. She had been doing that for twenty years. Artist, you know.

My house near the beach would be the starting point. It was a nice, small villa where I could reflect, and she could do her thing. It was early spring, and we could flower together. I rather liked our burgeoning closeness.

"What do you have planned today?" she asked the morning after arrival.

"I would like to walk the beach when it warms up outside, maybe about twelve," I told her.

"What happens for you when you do that?" she asked.

"Different things. I think about my mother, and gratitude."

"Gratitude?"

"Yes, she gave me a good life, a good foundation. She was a teacher. First graders."

"What else did she give you?"

"She was calm and sophisticated. She allowed herself and others to be themselves. She was not judgmental. She had opinions and principles that she lived by."

"Will you walk alone today?" she asked.

"Yes. What will you do today?" I asked her.

"I think I will go into town, catch a meeting and go to the bookstore for coffee and a feel."

"A feel?" I quizzed.

"Yes, feel the earth, the people, the vibe."

"And?"

"Just to feel it. Then I'll come back about three."

"Riding the bike?"

"Walking, I think. I could use the exercise."

"What will you do with the feeling today?"

"I don't know."

"Okay, we'll talk later."

"Yes."

I counted about sixteen people out walking when I got there. The oldest had to be about ninety-eight, a woman. I'm sure her escort was at least eighty. There were no teenagers this time of day, or many visitors. These were locals and I knew most of them. The retired agent was still hiding, the investor was on his phone, the drug dealer had changed gold necklaces, and the police chief had a new girlfriend. Sally Rutherford told me of her golf game, and that Bud had passed the day after Christmas. Ronny Jones said his knee felt better since the replacement surgery. Ida's face was holding up. I spoke to them all before setting up camp near the marshes by one thirty, I had walked a few miles and could sit and relax by then.

Carla called just as I sat on the wooden chaise with umbrella I had rented for the day. She told me of her feel and asked if I would write a poem about it coming up from the ocean. I told her I would.

Out around the last one said,

"the next time come but don't stay long."

"What does that mean?" Carla asked after dinner.

"Well you described a feeling of hope, and I think of the waves in the ocean as a coming and going, and sometimes, of course, the tide changes and moves higher or lower."

"So, is hope like that?"

"Only if not followed by a need for faith in something, or someone."

"Not the act?"

"No. The act is separate. The feeling is eternal."

"So, is that why I called?"

"No, that's why I answered. I hoped you were okay, but I had faith in our connection."

"To what?"

"To each other."

"How long will it last?"

"Until the next time."

REFLECTIONS FOR A TIME

I was dreaming that I was out running through the woods and the phone rang. "She died," Ginny said, "She died. Come on back home."

"Okay," I said.

It had been this time of year, and she was outside raking the dirt between the iron fence and the grass. It was a small area, but she was doing it. She will have surgery tomorrow to remove the cancer blocking her colon. She had not talked about her health much, but we knew she had lost weight and didn't get out as often. She had been a teacher, you know.

When I got to the hospital that afternoon, three days after surgery, when she had to be taken back because the stitching had come loose, she was finishing six scratch-off tickets she had been given by a friend.

She liked to gamble, and these were her favorites. I thought it odd for her to be doing that now but what else was she to do? She would die within an hour, and I saw the last movement in the breathing cup. I tried to move her foot back onto the bed, but it was stiff and returned to its last position each time. She was at peace and had seen all her family that day.

"I was glad when they said unto me, let us go into the House of The Lord Forever."

**

I could feel his emptiness from the past, a present day scarred by acts of war here and abroad. Jimmy Taylor wanted more from life than he had to give. His sweet regard for others was overshadowed by an experience of loss, or really, a never having peace. Somehow it was robbed from him early in life. Maybe his father never cared for him.

He had come to me for therapy, referred by a friend who had not had difficulties post-war, who had been able to develop a family life that supported his business success and civic participation. Farley was basic, a good person. Healthy in a way that shows forth not only in how he walks about, but in what he says about the way things are. They used to call that maturity.

Farley and Jimmy had grown up on the east side of town, low middle with a lot of hope. There was a general sense of place without any notions of advancing beyond a certain height, some places were for others to attend. Jimmy's folks were good with money and shared what everyone made through a common pot. The pains of the past were just that, pains from the past. The present was better as no one had been hanged in recent memory, and you didn't have to deal with too many white people in the neighborhood. At work was enough, Jimmy always said.

Jimmy came to my office not really knowing what to expect. I would take it easy with him as Farley had warned of an explosive temper that almost wound him up in the penitentiary. He would just go off sometimes. Friends had suggested he smoke pot, but he didn't like it. He wanted to stay natural. He rarely took medication of any kind and didn't really need to. He did, however, need to develop some new coping skills.

Walking into the office he gave off a bad vibe, a warning I rarely got with people who came in for counseling, whatever their issue. Something in the way he moved his neck startled me. Had he been injured as a child, abused perhaps? Something?

"Mr. Gregory?" he said coming into the waiting room.

"Yes, Thomas Gregory. How are you today?" I answer.

"Good. I'm a friend of Farley's. He told me to come see you."

"Yes, Farley's a good man. He told me you all are good friends."

"Yes, for forty years. Best friends."

"Okay, good, come on in and let's talk."

He looked around before sitting, seemingly to get comfortable with the space, and not looking for anyone. It took about ten seconds before he nodded to me that it was okay. He moved his head side to side popping his neck gently and asked how much this would cost. I said eighty an hour and he said okay. I hadn't seen a wad of money like that since the pool room days, but he peeled off four twenties and placed them on my desk. "Keep the receipts for me," he said. I said, "Okay."

"So, what I know is that my dad was not a tough guy. He seemed okay enough, but he didn't have a spark, that 'whoomph' we like to see. When I left home, it was to show that I had it," Jimmy started. "Still got it, but not lately."

"What's happened?" I ask.

"Okay, let's look at it this way..."

He talked with little pause for thirty-six minutes.

"So, we can work with that," I commented to him.

"Okay, so starting next week I'll finish the story, and you can tell me what it all means, right," he offers.

"I can give my impression," I said to him.

"And that's going to help me?" he asked solemnly.

"Only if we talk about the anger."

"Oh that, you've heard."

"Yes. Can you handle this sort of thing?" he asks me.

"Been there, done that," I give him the reference from the 90s.

"Good. It's a problem. Okay, I'll see you next week."

"Good. Same time."

"Her face was full and bright," he began when he returned the following week. "Handsome as it were, crème colored, with a softness to it, though I never touched her. Her voice rang to my ears singing a good morning, or how are you, sir, that christened an invitation to connection, would draw me out of my hole as I ordered two almond croissants and a coffee. I suspect she was ten years younger, and I wanted something from her, though whatever that is that keeps me hidden, alone, not sure, usually surfacing with women my age, so now I lunged into a fantasy of not what we could do, or have, but all the reasons it would not work, now that I had seen her fifty times over two years. Always the same, "how are you, sir. What can I get you?"

"Were you single during this time?" I asked him.

"No, married to my first wife. Happily, I thought. We divorced six years ago."

"Were you the same age?"

"Yes?"

"What happened?"

"Sir, I really can't say. We just started talking one day, after three years I think, and decided to do something else. She has since remarried I heard."

"So, the lady from the pastry shop?"

"Disappeared. I've been there for a month now, like before, and haven't seen her."

"Did you ask about her?"

"No."

"Would you like to see her again?"

"No, that was a moment in time. Nothing was to come of it. It was nice the way it was."

"How about from her end?"

"I would like to think something, but she was just a nice young woman going about the business of her duties, who happened to make my day lighter."

"We have not talked about anger?"

"No, I have none today."

"Next week?"

"Maybe?"

I went about my case files, making notes on Mr. Taylor and reflecting on my loss. She had been a full, wonderful lady and like most kids perhaps never knew the full breath of her life; but of course, how could I, she was momma? I was busy growing up, getting experience to train for this line of work. She was always there, the comfort, the love, the support, the smarts. So now she was gone, and I would have to make do with what she left me, a treasure trove of wonderful insights into human experience from a dedicated practitioner. I was truly blessed with a foundation to go on with the rest of it.

THE EVENNING

They were becoming good friends, but she wanted more from him. The dinner he prepared had been satisfying, and she felt comfortable lounging on the sofa in the den now that sexual urges were coming to the surface. She wasn't sure when he would approach her, but she hoped he was feeling the same way. At this age and stage of life it wasn't difficult to talk about the subject if need be, but she wanted things to progress without much conversation beyond the usual health considerations already discussed.

"Anything more to drink?" he asked, walking towards her, then stepping away from where she sat to get his glass of water.

"Not now, thanks."

He sat next to her and started on about retirement and how odd it feels not going to work each day as he had for forty years.

"It took me about four months," she offered.

"To?" he questioned.

"To get over the shock and realization that I had come to this point in life. It all seemed rather simple and easy looking back. One day I went to work at the hospital and here I am. Thirty-two years for me. It's like I can't remember what happened."

They both give a hearty laugh.

"That's what I've been feeling that I should remember more, or at least be ruminating over things done. I guess it means that it was all okay," he posits to her.

"Well, you know, no indictments, no major accusations of wrongs, I followed the professional code of ethics as best I could, I guess you did the same?"

"Yes. I guess that's a big part of it," he agrees. "No regrets."

"No, not at all. I gave it my best. Always!" she says.

"Yes, let's toast to that!"

He gets up to get her a glass with water, then decides to kiss her instead. It's awkward but they both smile at the move. It lingers, and further moves are made by both parties. He gestures to the bedroom, and she agrees.

The next morning he's up first sitting outside on the back deck which has a view into the city from the east. She joins him after pouring a cup of coffee. He's thinking about the last night he worked and had to kill a man.

"Good morning," she says.

"Good morning to you, how did you rest?" he asks.

"Well, thanks. How about you?"

"Good, I'm usually up early."

"What are you thinking about?" she asks him.

"Work. My last day of work."

"Was it just glad handing and saying goodbyes to people?" she asks not knowing.

"No, I was wrapping up a case and had to kill a man," he answers matter-of-factly.

"Oh, you had mentioned your work before, but I didn't think..."

"It was unusual."

"Okay, so, what are you doing today?"

"Thanks, but I can talk about it if you would like to hear it."

"No, I'm sorry. It's too early."

"That it is but maybe later."

"I'll just go back inside and let you think some more."

"Okay, sure, that's fine."

Susan shyly gets up from the chair and goes into the kitchen. He follows, and they caress gently.

"We can start over later," he says to her.

"Maybe," she answers as she goes into the bedroom to dress and go home.

Susan tried to describe her feelings when she called him about noon.

"They were new and jumbled," she said to Jack. "I guess it was too intimate after last night. I didn't want to get that close to you or remember my last night of work at the hospital. I was enjoying talking about being retired."

"What happened?" he asked her.

"Something similar. An overdose. A young man, 19. I should have saved him. I missed some things."

"Well we do have lots to talk about, don't we?"

"Yes. Dinner at my place tonight?"

"Yes," he agreed.

"Horace Griffin had been selling drugs since the 90s. He averaged a couple million a year net and had a good lifestyle. He was in a committed relationship with Donna Jenkins, and they lived on the outskirts of Atlanta. Horace, like so many of the heroin dealers still around from that era, never used the stuff himself. It was a product that made him and his runners lots of cash. His front was a commercial real estate business where he sold a few small buildings each year, but it was not something he gave a lot of time to. As a matter of fact, he would turn down most deals that came his way. What he loved to do was shoot pool with his friends, though he was a less than average player. What they talked about was baseball, and the homerun Horace hit to win the NCAA southwestern regional in 1980. It was stunning, and the high point of his life."

"I had been following him for two years and we were supposed to bust him the day before April 10. He had made a different move with a shipment of drugs, so we waited until the next day. My captain asked if I wanted off to relax on my last official day of duty, but I had to be there to see him go down. Horace was a slender, refined kind of guy and I think I wanted to rub his face into what he was about, a common drug dealer who helped ruin people's lives. We had never known him to carry a pistol, so I was surprised when he drew on me when I opened his car door. I literally shot him before I knew it," Jack shared.

"Wow, so much the same thing. This kid had come in, brought in by his daddy, who thought he was on some other drug, a hallucinogenic or something, so he didn't know the boy was an addict and had more drugs on him. The techs said they searched him, but as I was doing my last round there, he was, needle still in his arm, stiff as a board. We performed the standard revival methods, but he was too far gone. I, like you, probably should have been doing something else my last night of work. But there I was! Should we feel sorry or angry about it?"

"I don't think so. We both were highly trained and skilled professionals who had success. Perhaps those situations spoke to our humanity not our skill level."

"Humility?"

"Yes. Who we are who we would like to be? Were you judged harshly?"

"No. But the poor family. But you're right, that's the way it goes."

"I mean I shot that guy, and I didn't have to think. It was an automatic response based on hours of training."

"And it was him or you."

"Right, no regrets. I was surprised at the feeling, afterwards, however. I was a clerk in the service during Vietnam. I never saw combat or had to kill anyone. I would not want to do that again."

"Since then the hospital's doing more emergency room training, and I wrote a paper about investigative procedures for the 21st century. We were way behind the curve on that one. That young man should have lived."

"So, would you like me to cook the salmon?" he asked, moving around in the kitchen.

"Sure, I'll prepare the rice. Broccoli's done."

THEY DIDN'T SAY

I was out walking because the car was gone as were my other worldly possessions. It was April bright and windy, cool. It was Saturday and I would need to eat soon. The O&W would be open, I could start there. They knew me, and the food would be adequate, and whoever else was there at this time of day would probably be like me just coming to or needing to make that next right move. I looked in the window first and saw a couple of regulars, Little Larry and Johnnie Mo eating like mad men and talking over the first scheme for the day. Connie Stewart was over near where Wilson, the overnight cook was restocking plates and such, shifting clothing in place from her last trick. She would be going to her job soon at Davenport Trucking Company clocking in as Henry Ferguson, warehouseman. She has worked there since June of last year when she got out of prison. She had settled into her new life and was more careful now, especially around here.

O&W was the kind of fifties joint that had weathered the civil rights movement and the drug culture. It was small and clean, able to host about ten sitting patrons with takeout orders being hurled to and caught by Waymon or Olivia during the daytime hours and Wilson overnight. There was a family feel to the place as they were comfortable with most anybody who came in as long as they acted right. People would have all kinds of stuff in their pockets or bags, but I don't recall any shootings or major fights inside. There was a kind of reverence from all who walked in; you could feel it! The bright steel stools with black top cushions were sturdy enough and the large front window allowed for a street view as the hustle and bustle of the neighborhood passed by, students, workers, or players of all persuasions. You could get what you needed without much fuss. The police knew the area and the games played. There were limits, however, as to what could happen.

I chose one of the seats facing inward as the side stools around the u-shaped counter would have me looking out to see who passed by or would stand around for a moment or two. I was tired and just wanted something to eat with not too much stimulation. I nodded to all present as Waymon approached.

"Where you been?" he asked, knowing I had not been around for a while.

"You know, here and there," I answered.

"Yeah, we heard you went out of town."

"Business, you know."

"Yeah, we know. What are you having?"

"Let me get a couple of splits and fries, and a clear cola drink."

"You need some bubbles, huh?"

"Yeah, bubbles, my stomach's a little tight."

"Okay, grits?"

"No thanks."

"Okay, it'll be up in a minute. Good to see you man."

"Good to be here."

He smirked a little and turned to call out the order to Olivia. He flipped his pad to the next page and placed a take-out order called in earlier, "White girl flying," which was a white meat chicken sandwich. He went over to Johnnie Mo and Little Larry and got into a fast-paced conversation filled with laughter and knowing winks. They knew I had been in the county jail for sixty days. I should have just told him. There were not many secrets in this joint.

I did not hear Ms. Owens call my name as I was deep in thought about something else, "Mr. Sims, would you come up front and read one of your poems for the class?" she had asked. "Andrew!"

"Oh, I'm sorry ma'am, I was somewhere else," I replied.

"Come back to earth, we need you down here," she said to the gentle laughter of my classmates.

"Okay, I'll do it," I agreed and moved to the front of the class and wrote on the chalk board, "The Waste of Time" by Andrew Sims:

Then the girls came back home,

followed by boys who won the game.

We talked of how our fortunes changed,
with the addition of wonder man.
There was applause and Ms. Owens clapped as well.

I had always wanted to be known as a poet, not a criminal. I never could balance the two, or rather I had so much energy and varied interests it was hard to stay focused on just a literary pursuit. Athletics were easy, school was easy and social affairs were fun, so much so that I stayed later and out later and about getting into the kind of trouble the bad boys would. I became a bad boy by default, a leader, but not in the ways of common decency.

I did not like the nickname, but it was because I could do things ahead of my peers, good things at first, then the dark stuff. Not too dark, just out of bounds enough to where the street cred I developed led to a good, but short military career. There, as well, ahead of my peers, good soldier, bad dope fiend.

I sat thinking of these things knowing that the O&W had served its purpose for me, trouble was ahead if I stayed around here, so I ate my breakfast, said goodbyes, and headed down Tupelo Lane to visit Uncle Bobby, a mentor of sorts. Bobby had been to the 'chain gang' and came back a better person. He would be able to guide me to greatness as an artist, plus, help me become a better person as well.

"Hey, come on in, boy," he said as he opened the front door to his apartment. "I've been waiting on you to come by. Come on in, have a seat."

It seemed smaller now, as he did as well. It had been six years since we last spoke returning here after a visit to the city's art gallery. We had studied some original art by famous dead people and lunched on a salad he made for us. It was quite a stimulating afternoon as I recall, one to which I was inspired to write several poems over the next few days. He had told me, however, that I would have some more living, hard living to do if I wanted to achieve greatness. I would have to suffer and hurt people in ways I would never know, but it would be worth it if I survived and delivered the goods. But he had said, I did not have to choose greatness, I could just be good and have a decent life. But we both knew I had been chosen for the first choice.

"Why are you here today?" he asked, offering bread and water.

"I don't want to fall back."

"How was prison?"

"It was not prison just county jail," I corrected.

"How was prison?" he again asked.

"Oh, I see. The street life."

"Yes."

"Painful, but gratifying. I learned a lot. I think I'm ready now."

"To do what, write?"

"No, to live, then write."

"Isn't that what you've been doing?"

"No, that was existing. I'm ready to live now."

"Okay, first lesson, don't read poetry."

"Why?"

"It will confuse you. You must develop a new style and have a career that defines you to the world. Poetry is a product that may or may not sell."

"Do you have any suggestions?"

"When you leave here walk to the park at Five Points and ask someone for a job and take it. You will know who when you see her."

"Okay. When do I report back to you?"

"You don't. This is our last session."

Arlene Holmes was distraught at the slow pace of her research. She needed another set of eyes but had not been able to hire the right person. Two had left overwhelmed by the work and another was looking for something else from her. The cops had to be called to remove him from her 17th floor office overlooking the park. "Surely someone is out there," she was thinking on her way to lunch at the Mandarin Grille. She had almost been hit by a city bus crossing Broad

Street looking back at someone who had caught her attention. Jittery and flustered now she decided to go sit in the park and eat later. It was a nice day and time away from the problem may help her clear the rambling thoughts. She took a seat just off from the waterfall, near the bank's statue of a great businessman from another era. His foundation had built the park to its present large, inviting, and luscious state. People felt good about being here and part of the city life. There was a chess contingency near the central path to the college, and a pavilion for students or others to study and connect, there were the regulated food trucks and abundant garden area for the office or trade workers to eat and relax, there were walk paths, and comfortable places to stop and fellowship along the way. She knew the area well and could blend in to the daily eleven to two parades of humanity unnoticed and not bothered.

Andrew was tired from the six miles walk from Uncle Bobby's and took a seat near a woman about his age. She seemed nice enough but surely not the one as her facial contortions spoke of something he did not want to cross. She was dressed like a businessperson, but he turned his attention to the chess players about twenty yards away. They did look at each other briefly but were far enough away that it was not weird. She stood, looked again at him and he spoke, "Hello, my name is Andrew Sims, and I need a job."

"Hello Andrew, do you need a job or a career?"

"I don't know yet, but I need a job."

"What kind of work do you do? Oh, excuse me, Arlene, Arlene Holmes."

"Good to meet you Arlene. I can do a lot."

"Well, actually I need someone to help with some research I'm doing. Are you good with math and have a lot of patience?"

Andrew thought of his time in county lockup counting the days to discharge.

"Yes, I can count and wait."

"When can you start?"

"Today, now."

"So, who was the greater mathematician?" she asked him.

"Jesus," he answered. "Bread, fish, feeding the multitude, you know the story."

She paused at that answer. He asked her a question.

"So, how do I know you're legitimate? You're just a lady sitting in the park."

"While you sit and ponder whether, you can continue, minus a fortress."

"Okay, so you know poetry."

"'And Sorrow Comes Along with Relief,' 1976, the year he left college to write poetry," she answers.

"Okay, good, how much do you pay?"

"I don't know, what do you need?"

"Enough."

"Okay. You're hired."

"Okay, I'm ready to start."

EDGE OF TOWN

They were dusty, smelly, and tired, the three brothers who landed on my doorstep Saturday, March 5, 1965. I had been in a preparation class all day and Phyllis was due at eight. We were getting ready for the March on Atlanta next Tuesday and I was getting supper ready when I heard the loud thump on the front porch. I grabbed the wooden chair close to me as a weapon and noticed the lights race pass the small kitchen window as the car sped away. I listened for a crash sound, or the smell of gas. Neither happened, just a gentle tap on the aluminum screen door by the older boy, Paul. I took a few steps, looked around the corner to the living room and heard a voice say, "one more time." I crept up on the front door, looked behind me for strength, and prayed. I still had the chair in my right hand, set it down and opened the door, three small black faces looked up to me and smiled, then stood in unison.

They didn't speak but Eugene, the next oldest boy, stepped forward and offered a handshake. Donovan did the same as Paul reached in his back pocket and gave me the folded sheet of paper. I took it and read it: "They need a home. Please help them. Charlotte."

I didn't quite know what to do next except let them in. Paul lifted the medium-sized suitcase and walked by me as I gestured for them to come in. They stood together until I told them to sit down. They did and looked directly at me. It was time to start a conversation, and I did.

Sitting in my sixth-floor office waiting for the football player to arrive for his session I thought of that evening wishing Paul and Donovan were still alive. I owed my success to them and the man who took us in, Avery Ragsdale. My brothers had died of drug overdoses ten years ago and Mr. Ragsdale lived to be seventy-two and had managed my practice until he retired seven years ago. I felt a sudden aloneness that was new especially since I had just been awarded the Counselor of The Year Award for my service to members of the community by offering free group therapy once a week to seniors who had recently lost a loved one. Maybe it was because I was going on vacation in a week and probably should have gone a month ago as I was feeling the stress of the burden of others, 'burn out' they used to call it. Now it's 'Care Giver Fatigue' or some such thing. At any rate I was ready to go until the doorbell rang. The person was obviously anxious, or in a hurry as they pushed the doorbell again rather quickly, I thought. I knew it was not my scheduled client, so I prepared for a challenge.

"Mr. Jones," the lady spoke when I let her into the reception area. "Eugene Jones, I've wanted to meet you for a long time. How have you been?" she asked, taking liberties.

"Whoa, slow down," I said to her. "Who sent you here?" I asked.

"Charlotte Hawkins, my sister, she said if I ever needed a friend to come to see you. By the way, I have something for you, it's an envelope she left in her will. She died last month of Leukemia. Here, take it, it's for you."

"Of course, come in, sit down, relax," I said trying to stay calm.

"Yeah, she knew you turned out well, and what happened to your brothers. Well, my husband died a junkie, stupid joker, alcohol too. Well. I'm going to go. I know where you are and when I need to talk to somebody I'll come back. Do I have to pay you?"

"Ma'am..."

"Okay, I'll see you. Read the letter. Bye"

She got up and left. I stood there with the letter, befuddled about what just happened. Before I could act the doorbell rang again, it was my client.

Frank Morton had been a defensive back and played in two super bowls. He was thick and muscular five years after retiring from football at the age of thirty. He was referred to me post inpatient treatment for a pain pill addiction. He was doing well a month into our sessions, and we were getting used to each other even though the conversation was still about the using, not core issues. I sensed he was ready today, and he stayed on the surface until I asked about his father.

"He was not there for us. He split, or they broke up when I was very young, probably four. I don't have much memory of him."

"How has that played out?"

"Really, only as a void, I guess. Always seemed my playmates had something I didn't, the ones whose father was present."

"You mean in the home?"

"That, or even if they just saw them ever so often. I had nothing. Well, I did have an uncle who was there for me. But I don't think that's the same."

"No. How does that make you feel?"

"Like a citizen of the world with no home."

"Part of the village?"

"Not really. It's the accountability factor. I've never felt I had to answer to anyone, so the feeling would be distant."

"Even with the football success not a full man?"

"Exactly. He's still living but we don't talk. Just never have."

"Would you like to?"

"There was a time, a few years back when I wanted to, but nothing happened. There was really nothing to ask or say. So, no. The issue is the void, not him."

"Very good," I said to him. "So, the drug use filled the void?"

"Never. The drugs were about the physical pain, period, a blocking dose they call it. The void just sits there, with or without the drugs. It's an emotional deficit."

"How about peer relationships?"

"The same."

"Lonely?"

"Ulmm. I don't know?"

"A void there too?"

"Yep."

When Mr. Morton left my thoughts returned to getting away. I deferred opening the letter for another day.

Donovan died first; he had been holed up in his apartment shooting dope for several hours after the police tried to serve him an arrest warrant. When they finally broke in, he was dead from the overdose of heroin and cocaine.

He had been a player, six kids by three mothers, and didn't provide a dime of child support. He had game, but no care. I knew who they were and made small gestures from time to time but had no relationship with my younger brother the last few years of his life. Eight years in prison didn't teach him discipline or respect. He was a drug addict and died that way.

Paul, on the other hand, died three months after Donovan. Family man, three great kids, his wonderful wife Julie, had a good life due to his skills as a salesman. His one-night affair with a British woman ended with them both dead from injecting 46% pure heroin after a company gathering in Aruba. It was his first time for both events. To his credit, he had done well and left his family comfortable enough to continue life in the manner to which they were accustomed.

I waited until the third day of vacation to open the letter. I wasn't quite relaxed yet and still had an emotional edginess going on. Mr. Ragsdale hadn't told us much, only that he took us in that night on faith, and a desire to do the right thing. He had raised us as best he could, and I was grateful.

"Eugene, I have been near enough to the three of you that I know what has happened. It's very sad to me about your brothers. They will never know what I have left for you as to why you all were abandoned that night, on that porch. Yes, I am your mother, and I just had to get away from the responsibility. I never married your father, and I was tired. I knew who Mr. Ragsdale was and what he was about so I put trust in him to do the right thing. He didn't know who I was, and I never contacted him. I don't have anything else to say except thank you for the life you have. Your Mother, Charlotte."

I didn't quite know what to do with this information. I really wish I had not gotten it! I would never meet her, and my brothers would never know even this tidbit. Okay, life goes on. I think I'll go for a swim and see where that takes me spiritually.

As I swam, I thought of the three million dollars Dexter Hollis left with me. He had two more years to serve on his eight-year sentence and we had lost contact. He had become a victim of 'diesel therapy' and was moved around to six different federal prisons for disciplinary reasons. He usually wrote or called a least every two months or so, but it was going on eight months now without a word. Secretly I hoped he was dead, or had done something to get more time, a lot more time; but those thoughts were fleeting and random. He had left the money with me because we were friends, and I had a certain level of trustworthiness. I was living just fine on my own money and the fee I charged him for keeping his money safe. I was not a criminal yet!

Thinking back on the letter, and my reduced sense of stress, I could begin to realize the new life ahead for me. I was fifty-three and Christina was back from her studies in Rome. We could sell the downtown condo and move to our cottage in Clarkeston. When she called, I did not answer. I sent a text back stating I was busy and would call in an hour. She responded with an I love you symbol.

It was the fall of 1988 when I first noticed Donovan was bad off on the stuff. He had a beard and wore the same clothes for days. He had gotten beat up a couple of times and had scars on his face. He looked weak and removed when I went to the hospital to see him after a call from his girlfriend of the day.

"Mr. Jones, his room is down here, 108," the nurse told me and pointed down a long hallway to the right side. I thanked her and moved in that direction. Before I got there, he was walking out with his bag of stuff, a change of clothes and some toiletries.

"Where are you going, buddy," I spoke, not really feeling the love for him now.

"None of your business," he responded.

"Can we talk for a minute?" I asked him as he stopped to look at me.

"No, I'm in a hurry. Talk to Linda, she knows everything. She should not have called you anyway. I'm all right. Just don't worry about me," he spoke with an air of arrogance.

"Okay, maybe another time?"

"Just don't worry, I'm okay."

With that he brushed past me and crept to the stairway exit. The female nurse chased him for a short distance but knew she had to let him go. We talked for a few moments, and she pulled his chart and made the necessary notes. I thanked her and left the facility. Walking outside I saw Donovan's car in the emergency parking area with a flat tire and in need of a good washing.

Christina sounded glad to hear from me, and I was glad to hear her voice. My head was clearing, and my body felt calmer.

"Hey darling, boy what a day!" I said to her.

"Oh yeah, what's up?" she asked.

"Just debriefing. I forget how stressful counseling can be."

"Well, you're very good at it and your clients love you."

"Thanks."

"We got an offer on the condo, it's above asking," she informs me.

"How much?"

"Ten, well eight thousand really. They're not asking for anything. They were there when the Butlers were and heard them talking. They knew it would not stay on the market long."

"Good job."

"Thanks. I'll be coming down tomorrow about four."

"Good. Anything else?" I ask.

"Just that I love you very much."

"Yes, I love you just as much. Thank you"

EPILOGUE

"Well, Mr. Larry Fleming, is there anything else to discuss?" Dr. Scott asked to wrap up their counseling session.

"No, I think I have cleared the desk, as it were. I'm ready to move on. Thanks."

Also by George H. Clowers, Jr.

All That We Are After
The Writer's Playground: Short Stories
The Moon Is My Confessor
The Case for Larry Fleming
Theft by Taking: A Fictional Memoir
I Wish to Hear the Autumn Wind
A Place, Then Nowhere
If You Have Nothing Better to Do...
I Paint, He Writes: Life Together
Book II and Others
Long Time to Sunset

Watch for more at https://www.georgeclowers.com.

About the Author

Retired substance use disorder counselor.
Read more at https://www.georgeclowers.com.

Milton Keynes UK
Ingram Content Group UK Ltd.
UKHW040256181024
449757UK00001B/69